Idols with Tears

Michael Fayia Kallon

Sierra Leonean Writers Series

Idols with Tears

ISBN: 978-9988-8779-2-7

Sierra Leonean Writers Series
Warima/Freetown/Accra
120 Kissy Road, Freetown, Sierra Leone
Kofi Annan Avenue, North Legon, Accra, Ghana
Publisher: Prof. Osman Sankoh (Mallam O.)
publisher@sl-writers-series.org
www.sl-writers-series.org

Other Books by Michael Fayia Kallon

The Ghosts of Ngaingah
'The Kissi Story Teller – Folktales from Sierra Leone
The Traffic Supervisor at JFK
Walking with a Cane: New York City's Food Stamps War

***Website*: www.makonabooks.com**
Facebook: MAKONA BOOK CLUB, INC.

INTRODUCTION

Michael Kallon is a native of Sierra Leone, West Africa, and has been in the United States on political asylum for nearly two decades. This long separation from his homeland must certainly be difficult and painful, but in the pages of *Idols with Tears,* it is evident that his memory and love of his country are strong; the passing years have not eroded his identification with Sierra Leone.

Nevertheless, Kallon's primary identification is not with Sierra Leone, in particular, but with his people, the Kissi, one of the many ethnic groups in the region whose history stretches back long before the European colonial period.

The fact that *Idols with Tears* is the first book to be written about the Kissi people is at the heart of Kallon's sense of its importance. For Americans (and, no doubt, Europeans), the significance of this can be blurred by historical representations of Africa and resulting media representations, which have portrayed and continue to depict Africa almost exclusively in terms of the nation states which grew out of colonial occupation.

In commenting on the assertion that Liberia, a neighbor of Sierra Leone on the West Coast of Africa, was founded by former liberated American slaves in the nineteenth century, Kallon has said to me, with due incredulity, that "Liberia was there long before the nineteenth century."

By fundamentally ignoring the much older ethnic nations, which had defined themselves long before the arrival of Europeans as colonizers, these representations belie the complexity of African history and cannot, in consequence, but distort what Africa is.

In addition to its importance as the first book to be published about the Kissi, *Idols with Tears,* in its emergence from a Kissi (as opposed to a Sierra Leonean, West African, or African) perspective, it is important as a corrective antidote to many of the reductive and inaccurate perceptions of Sierra Leone and Africa in general, which plague American and European (mis)understanding.

Idols with Tears is a story Kallon often heard repeated (and rumored to be true) as a child growing up; the love affair between Kumba and Tamba takes place somewhere between 1910 and 1920.

What of this story?

From an ethnographic perspective, it is of considerable interest. Funeral ceremonies, courtship and marriage customs, religious beliefs, gender roles, social structure, food resources: all are depicted here in meticulous, engaging, and vivid detail. While the bulk of the story takes place before either Christianity or Islam had made substantial inroads into Kissi culture, the closing section provides a Kissi perspective on the Christian and Muslim's first arrival, which is also of considerable ethnographic interest.

At the same time, I am generally a bit uncomfortable with foregrounding "ethnographic interest" to an extreme degree in this book, due to the long and detailed history in our academic/intellectual sphere of turning storytelling into scientific specimen. Stories laid out on tables dissected and probed for "evidence" of theories which all too often have very little to do with the people who told—and continue to tell the stories.

This story is not an ethnographic study, though Kallon's choice to write a Kissi story rather than a "study" of the Kissi as the first book about his people is itself of ethnographic significance.

Kallon himself takes on the role of storyteller with *Idols with Tears*, and in this role, the Kissi oral tradition provides his core foundation. The sympathetic reader will find a refreshing absence of the kinds of earmarks which characterize just a little too much of our (Western) self-consciously "creative" writing. The narrative is direct, organized in clear dramatic blocks, as the characters are simultaneously painted in broad vivid strokes. The narrative voice carries the resonance of the spoken word; that English is not Kallon's first language is evident in the idiosyncratic nature of his wording, which heightens the implicit suggestion of orality: English being made a vehicle for Kissi storytelling.

Kallon did not create or invent this story: it is the narrative of events which occurred nearly ninety years ago, which subsequently entered Kissi oral tradition, the medium through which he came to know it in his childhood nearly three decades later. In setting the story down in writing he is extending his role of storyteller by bringing the story of Tamba Kolloh and Kumba Mongor to a non-Kissi audience. He is aware of his audience: American readers. Hence the rich abundance of detail: much that would be assumed knowledge to native listeners, needs explanation and elaboration in order to be understood American readers who (like myself) are entering into a part of the Kissi world for the first time.

Idols with Tears is not without some difficulties for the reader who takes certain European and American narrative conventions for granted, namely the difficulty of some of the transition passages between major scenes in the story. They are not always clearly linked by a linear chronology, though a chronology is clear in a progression of the scenes themselves. Some scholars of African oral tradition note that the African conception of time is very different from the closely measured, clock based European conception of time. I see this same difficulty in some of the transition passages in the versions of the *Malian Epic of Sonjara* by Bamba Suso and Banna Kanute, in the versions translated by Gordon Innes. It is pertinent to note that *Sonjara* is indigenous to the broad cultural region of which the Kissi are a part, and Kallon knows it as a part of his cultural heritage. I might speculate that the difficulties in the presentation of chronology reflect what some scholars of African oral traditions suggests represents a conception of time which is manifested in emphasis in a series of clusters around important events, rather than an emphasis on measured chronological time. This may take some readers getting used to, but the sympathetic reader will find perseverance rewarded.

Ultimately, what remains is the story, and the world Kallon so lovingly describes: the moving story of Tamba Kolloh and Kumba Mongor; the funeral ceremony for Kumba's father Nyuma Mongor enlivened by their tricksterish humor of the Bolah; the scouring of the village of forces which threaten its internal integrity; the non-judgmental portrayal of the arrival of Islam and Christianity as unduly alien forces; and, enveloping all of this, the vividly detailed daily life of the Kissi.

Jamie Williamson, Professor
Burlington College
May 20, 2004

PREFACE

Idols with Tears, is the first book written on the Kissi culture. The Kissi are found in Sierra Leone, Liberia, and in Guinea-Conakry on the west coast of Africa. One of the most incredible aspects of the Kissi is how they select a village medicine-man, herbalist, or a chief priest. The ghost of Nyuma Mongor, (who had been considered a renowned psychic and a deity among them), mysteriously chooses Tamba Kolloh, the fictitious character in this work.

Tamba Kolloh's ardent love for Kumba Mongor is also the talk of the village. Together they organize the Poro society for boys and the Sande society for girls. They pour libation to their forebears and make sacrifices at the oracles and the shrines for special reasons. And with mysterious incantations, they also wipe the tears of the idols.

The book is written on the Kissi of Sierra Leone who are also great farmers, wonderful hunters, and mysterious reapers. They are also very productive natives; and the book also tells about how they launched a – witch-hunt, harvesting on the rice farms, courtship, stories as narrated by their illustrious griots, burial ceremonies, the pouring of libation to appease the gods; the launching of Poro and Bondo societies, native songs and *dances* – *w*ith fun and mischief. Some of these mysteries faded with time as strange cultures clashed with those of the Kissi.

For even to this day, the advent of Christian, and Moslem beliefs, discouraged the Kissi from such spiritualism – and, the idols lie dormant with not enough chief priests to wipe their tears. At the back of this work, you will be acquainted with a glossary of unfamiliar terms and expressions in the Kissi dialect, interpreted in English. It's hoped that you will enjoy reading this first book on the Kissi culture. These are experiences etched in my memory since childhood.

Michael F. Kallon
Author
August 24, 2002
New York City
U S A

ACKNOWLEDGEMENTS

I am indebted to Mrs. Sarah Woolford, living in Richmond Virginia, US~ who discovered my talent as a writer and poet at the Kakata Teachers' College in Liberia, West Africa, from 1999 to 1980.

To my late sister, Ms. Jeneh M. Kallon, who resided in New York, U.S., for sponsoring my migration to the United States of America just to escape the ethnic massacre that engulfed Liberia and later Sierra Leone from 1980s to 1990s.

To Ms. Denise Bert, her daughter Tasha, and little Darcel, these are the kindest and most generous people I know for their patience with my constant presence in their home in New York City.

To my mother, Madam Finda N. FORYOH-Kallon, also in New York City, U.S; it was really you, Mom, who, through your hardships to bring us up as a single mother in Koindu, in the Kissi Bendu Kingdom in Sierra Leone, on the West Coast of Africa, taught us that perseverance is the key to success.

To the director, professors, and the entire staff of Burlington College in Vermont, U.S.; this is a clear outcome of the dynamic work done by all of you, the very gifted men and women of this illustrious college.

Especially to Professor Jamie Williamson, your very relentless guidance and tireless efforts made this work a success. To all the old and the new students of this unique college, be very proud of them, and also be very proud of this work.

To Mrs. Swadu Mansaray–Kallon, you greased my elbow and encouraged me to finish this story. Thank you for your kindness, love, and human understanding.

To Junior, Brenda, Hawah, Edward and Zanaria - Kallon, it's an invitation that I am sending to you to read some of the experiences I grew up with, still etched in my memory in the midst of the most famous hunters, ancient warriors, and psychics, and great farmers. These are a very mysterious sect of natives of the Kissi tribe of Sierra Leone on Africa's West Coast.

Also, in memory of my late daughter Margaret Kumba Kallon...

EDITOR'S NOTE

Through *Idols With Tears*, I have come to encounter the Kissi people as a culture in search of truth, happiness, solidarity, communion and beauty. They are truly a people who live to experience the range of human emotions: from passion, to disdain for untruth, from heightened spirituality, to finding extreme pleasure in the utterly ridiculous and humorous—they are an exuberant tribe. It was a tremendous pleasure to lend my editorial affection to this unique and wonderful gift to the American public—our first intimate recorded knowledge of the Kissi and their traditions.

Kallon's narrative is a clash between Sierra Leonean tribal oral tradition and a timeless universal love story. Together, we witness a bond of devotion between a man and a woman living a stable, principled and faithful life in honor of the kinsmen/women who have come before. Their efforts to preserve and uphold the ancient sacred rites and rituals of the Kissi culture left a lasting impression for generations to come.

Kallon shines in his true light as Kissi storyteller, historian, sociologist and writer—all efforts executed with extreme joy, giving meaning, fullness and life to his country, heritage, culture and people.

Music plays a unique role in the Kissi culture. Sometimes, it is used for certain types of communication. Kallon interweaves music throughout his narrative. The reader is present in the village square as Yamba, the griot, tells his story and the crowd roars in response.

Kallon's narrative, like the Kissi music, does not necessarily have a melody, but rather a rhythmic sound—with much drumming and whistling—his story is told with the rhythm, fluidity and cacophony that is reflected in the colorful culture of his people.

Though the Kissi culture and tradition have changed with the years, Kallon reawakens the Kissi's not so distant past; a past that, if it had not been recorded here, could have been lost forever.

Although Christian and Muslim foreigners moved in on the Kissi in order to "convert" them from their "barbaric polytheistic ways," the Kissi treated all kinds of foreigners with respect. The Kissi were a faithful and loyal people who adhered to their ancestral customs and beliefs with the utmost of respect and integrity, as the times, and their country, continued to change.

Blessings Michael! May this be the first of many Kissi annals to come.

Christie Dennis
Editor, October 10, 2004
New York, New York

CHAPTER ONE

The whirlwind blew dry leaves and debris tremendously, engulfing parts of Yilandu village, as dusk was about to fall. A rainbow arched halfway in the clear sky. Children, some half-naked and with bare feet, were with the old, gathered around logs of fire. The elders drank cups of fresh palm and bamboo wine from kegs the tappers had collected from the trees. Palm wine came from the dry land, and the bamboo wine from the bamboo tree in the swamp. They called the wine "from God to man," which meant it actually required no fermentation; they drank it in its natural state.

Half-naked and barefoot children played *Duduleng* while their elder brothers played *Weiyoh*. The girls played by clapping both hands against each other, and stepping with intricate techniques, to fit the dance that accompanied the game. All enjoyed the blessings of the moonlight as it illuminated the village with a placid durability. A few among them sat in smaller groups to listen to stories narrated to them by their elders. The elders narrated stories of the might and valor of their ancient heroes who fought the baboons on the Ngebadu Hill and of the idols that performed mysterious deeds, which no human being could dare perform today.

Tamba Kolloh had just returned home after picking nuts from his late grandfather's kola nut tree and entered his hut with a basketful or full basket? He had been accompanied by his fiancée Kumba Mongor, but they had not entered the village together. She had taken a different footpath so that the villagers wouldn't recognize any traces of illicit passion on their faces.

It was under the same tree that they had talked about how they loved each other. They never kissed, as it was considered a taboo in their culture. She was a beautiful and charming young woman. She had slim legs that made her a target for most of the other young men in the village, and even in the clan. They set snares to attract her attention at makeshift roadblocks, and at the creek side where she was sure to go every day—since it was the only source of drinking water, and also used for laundering in the village.

When humidity was high during the day, the boys went to bathe in the Pelia stream, or some traveled as far as to the Dakar stream, on the outskirts of Kpangbening village—a considerable distance from Yilandu. As the cock crowed early in the morning, the boys and the young women in Yilandu went to fetch water from the creek. The water was used for cooking and for washing the wooden spoons, calabashes and clay pots. The young women had to boil the water so that their husbands could bathe with it.

Tadanpoli was among the most renowned country cloth weavers in the Toli clan. Kumba had walked by his hut. Cloth was manufactured from cotton thread in tortoise shells spun on short sticks by the old woman spun. Once the villagers could gather enough thread, it was then given to the old men in the village who weaved them into a neatly intricate pattern they called Kola-makissio (Kissi country-cloth).

Early in the morning, Tadanpoli brought his local cottage-weaving machine outdoors. It was made of two long sticks into which a comfortable seat was made. He then mounted it behind his hut, under a pear tree, which provided shade. Under the canopy of the pear tree, he enjoyed the gentle waft in the day and a cool breeze in the evening. There he pedaled his weaving machine and at the same time passed the thread into a round shuttle, a skill that yielded a neatly intricate pattern. The factory was outdoors and the operation only stopped when black clouds gathered in the sky and then made thunderous noises to conjure rainy storms. Tadanpoli knew that the clouds predicted a downpour of rainfall. Sometimes droplets of water signaled an immediate rainfall.

Even at Tadanpoli's weaving industry, the young men in the village awaited Kumba Mongor, whose beauty dazzled them so much. The old man knew, for he had already experienced such youthful escapades. There he sat and shook his gray head to the rhythm of their youthful antics. He slowly sang melodious songs of old and narrated funny jokes and stories, which not only impressed the young men and women, but also, encouraged them to come to visit him under the spreading pear tree.

He was one of the old men in the village gifted with such talent. He never stopped his work although he got entangled in the laughter. He could suck his toothless mouth violently, with a quiver of a smile. Yet, although the children enjoyed the faces he pulled, he appeared to ignore them all. Kumba Mongor loved Tadanpoli, and he was also her comedian. He spotted her as she returned.

"Oh! Kumba, as the rosy tints of dawn touch the eastern horizon of Yilandu, you will receive a sad message," he predicted.

He could predict the future, too. He was one of the Toli clan's most trusted psychics.

Kumba Mongor now concentrated her energy and power to prove to Tamba Kolloh her love. This then encouraged him to strive harder, to win her as wife—the rumor of which was already in all corners of the village. The villagers had returned to their various homes from their farms. It was now pitch dark and the countryside was very dangerous.

"Um-humm," Tamba Kolloh mused. "My grandfather Bandakillie Fugbu, who once lived in Yilandu, used to tell my mother that when one sees a rainbow arch over a village, it signifies that a chameleon is giving birth in a swamp or in the bushes near the village."

Kumba Mongor had secretly escaped from her mother's hut, and surreptitiously gone to Tamba Kolloh's hut. This was how she paid him surprised visits.

"Well Tamba, sometimes the rainbow means that a chameleon has opened its mouth in the swamp. That was what my dad told me on the farm," she said calmly.

"Um-humm Kumba, but maybe it also signifies some sad omen in the village or clan."

"Eh!" both of them agreed with cheerful grins on their faces. They remained silent briefly. Kumba Mongor thought over it very seriously.

"Like what strange incident, Tamba?" she queried.

"Uum-mm Kumba, I have been hiding this from you. It may also predict the death of one of most venerable elders in the clan," he concluded sadly.

She got concerned. Her father was now seriously ill.

Kumba Mongor's father was regarded as one of the most renowned psychics, a witch doctor, a sorcerer, gifted herbalist, high priest, and a deity in the clan. He had saved lots of lives, especially the innocent children and babies, from the claws of some of the most deadly invincible idols, like the *Sambeiyoh (a deadly god that kills instantly),* and the witches.

"His death would mean the lives of the innocent ones would then be at the mercy of those atrocious men and women who injured them as they go on their rampant sprees of destroying human lives," Tamba Kolloh concluded sadly.

"Um-humm," both of them agreed together.

Kumba sat down in a slumberous mood in a raffia chair and pondered quietly. It was during the farming season and her father had perfectly laid acres of farmland on the Ngebadu Hill, on the outskirts of Yilandu. When his sickness first started, they thought that he was suffering from trifling cold. But his entire body ached, his speech blurred, and soon his sudden sickness drew everyone's attention in the village. The villagers were greatly astounded. They stood speechless in smaller as well as in larger groups—all focusing on the old man's sickness. Some of them prayed that the God Almighty may pour His blessings on him. Even the children sat sadly as the elders told of his exploits and audacious deeds in their village. They also thought of the great calamity that was surely going to fall on them if the old man were to die.

The whirring of countless insects in the village and the

surrounding bushes contaminated the midnight's atmosphere.

Tamba Kolloh bowed over her, and her round charming face was smiling and receptive as always.

"Oh! Meleka (God), spare my poor father's life," Kumba Mongor cried pathetically.

They were together. For the first time, he played with her breasts and drew her gently to the wooden bed, which was neatly decorated with dry grass that looked like sponge. The grass was cut from the swamp, dried and used as a mattress. On it, was a newly weaved country-cloth. She lay comfortably and for the first time confessed to Tamba Kolloh that most of the young men in the village made advances on her and had voiced their liking for her, and had chased her to the creek and also to old man Tadanpoli's weaving industry under the giant pear tree.

Some of them had been very rude to her too. Yet, though sexual harassment was not a punishable crime in their culture, the elders never allowed the young men to play with the women, especially virgins, in that very rude manner. Sometimes, the young men who indulged in such rude activities were summoned to the chief's decision making shed and advised to stop. If they did not, appropriate action was taken to discourage such acts.

Kumba couldn't look directly into Tamba's eyes. She felt guilty about what she was doing with her boyfriend since her mother hadn't given her the permission. It was the first time she lay on a man's bed. She lay on her back and looked directly at the ceiling and mud wall.

As for Tamba Kolloh, he looked at her bravely and

touched her gently. She enjoyed it when he touched her breasts. They lay and discussed their future as husband and wife. They heard the little puppy whining for food in the hut. The expressions on their faces suggested that they were to engage in a consensual sex for the first time in their lives. In such a very strict culture, making each other naked or having sex was done absolutely in secrecy and in darkness. It also meant that after she had been initiated into womanhood, she was surely going to conceal it.

Tamba then extinguished the flames from the bottle lamp, which produced clouds of smoke in the hut. They made themselves naked and Tamba Kolloh lay on her calmly. She tried to resist at first, since she was a virgin, but within a few minutes, she had lost her virginity and became very brave. She did not stay in the bed with him that night.

He accompanied her to her mother's hut in the early hours of the morning. By then, the moon had faded away.

When her frightened mother opened the door, she screamed, "Gboh-gboh-gboh-Kumba!" with fear. "Where are you coming from?" she yelled out loudly. "Don't you know that this is the most sinister and dangerous hour in the morning?" she cried incessantly.

Her mother then disclosed that the night air was chilly and that the evils were angrily passing by and even the owls hooted, and the bush babies cried in a distance.

She then whispered to her, "Do you know that cannibals caught a little boy in another village just a few miles from here?"

Tamba Kolloh had hidden behind the large leaves of a banana plant where only Kumba could see him. They heard the guard dogs growling very rudely at the erratic flight and the noises of nocturnal insects, and especially the noises from the dark bushes. It's believed in the culture that the dogs do see invincible beings that human beings couldn't see.

"*Ndeh*! (Mother), I was at my grandpa's hut. I just decided to come to your hut after I had a terrifying dream. In the dream, I saw cannibals with very long knives and they had masks on their faces, and they were chasing me," she said lying.

Her mother then nodded with keen eyes and shook her head gently sideways. She didn't take her word.

"Kumba! You are not really telling me the truth," she asserted.

She then advised her never to come home at that time of the morning, especially when the air was full of great danger. Adding, she wouldn't be able to sleep again, since her daughter had woken her abruptly from her very precious sleep, ending with telling her that it was their custom to marry, especially to the man who knew her first. They never encouraged their children to become prostitutes in the village, and especially when the bride price was so high.

However, Kumba Mongor didn't hear a word her mother said, immediately as her body touched the bed, she was unconsciously knocked down by a heavy sleep. She was tired from her first physical encounter with Tamba Kolloh that night and felt that he was a fine, generous, and a sympathetic young man.

As soon as Tamba saw that she had entered into her

mother's hut, he vanished into the darkness and went back to his hut.

Early the next day, he hurriedly awoke and went to the forest near the village to see if one of his snares had caught any animals that roamed the night. On one of the snares, he met a trapped bulky groundhog, which had died over night. He quickly picked some giant leaves and wrapped the dead animal inside, tying it neatly with cords he loosed from the gigantic trees that stood nearby. Tamba rushed to Yilandu and went to Kumba Mongor's mother's hut. There he made a very respectful presentation to her for the first time.

"*Ndeh-Eseh.*" (Good morning, Mom.)

"Hum- Tamba, *A-cho-keNdeh*? (Are you alright, Tamba?)

"Eh! *Ndeh.*" (Yes, Mom.) She had noticed that he had been very friendly lately with her daughter. Everyone admired him greatly in the village. They loved him, too. It was in fact an honor for him to pay such a respect to her. Yet, she was very terrified by the great kindness that he showed her that day as he presented the entire dead animal to her.

"Ah! Tamba, *Balikah.*" (Thank you.)

"*Balikah.*"

"*Balikah*, Tamba," she said repeatedly.

"Kumba! Kumba!" she yelled continuously, but her daughter never answered.

Kumba had hidden inside her mother's hut. She had gone simply to vanish from their sight because she was so ashamed that she had lied to her mother, and she couldn't lay her eyes on Tamba. Kumba had undertaken a secretive escapade that was surely going to change her world significantly.

For the first time, her mother started to wonder about her whereabouts at the time she disappeared from home, though she loved her daughter's boyfriend for his boldness and marvelous air of pity.

Tamba sat comfortably on a wooden and fork-like stool. He leaned his back in the position so that he could see directly inside the hut in front of him. Kumba Mongor could see him directly from the small openings that penetrated the mud wall, only visible to someone in the hut as the rays of the sun penetrated through them.

"Kumba-eh!" her mother yelled for the last time.

"Eh! *Ndeh*," Kumba finally answered politely in a very calm manner, customary in the Kissi culture.

Kissi children never shouted at the elders. They obeyed their mothers and fathers, and bowed to greet elders too.

"Please come outside, you stupid fool," her mother said angrily.

When Kumba appeared, she stood with her head to one side. Her pose was dignified but unconsciously provocative.

"Look, Kumba, this is what your *ponornum (husband)* brought for us today," she joked judiciously.

Kpannah Mongor was not contented in her daughter's appearance; yet, she stood with the high color in her fat cheeks, frail and harmless. From the moment, she uttered *ponornum*, Tamba Kolloh was now positively intrigued, and for the first time, he understood that she was going to be his wife. He now sat arrogantly and noticed the serene honesty in his would be mother-in-law's fat face.

Kumba Mongor looked imploringly at her mother and

bent down her small and very beautiful blue eyes. She did though portray a cheerful grin on her face, which beamed proudly as the sun was now rising to light the azure sky. Tamba and Kumba exchanged exuberant jokes, and he bade them goodbye by bowing his head respectfully as he left. Kumba then entered into her mother's hut and slept for hours. She had never before lied to her mother. She thought about it seriously.

Later, Chokah, a boy from the village rushed to her. She woke up tiredly. He told her that Tamba Kolloh had sent him to tell her to meet him under the kola nut tree. Kumba blinked her eyes faintly and noticed the honesty in the little boy's face. She felt dizzy and lay helpless, telling him in a very sluggish manner to go ahead and that she was going to be there within a few minutes. Chokah, who had mastered the job of an emissary, rushed jokingly to Tamba Kolloh and disclosed that she had agreed to come.

Where Tamba stood in a small bush around the village, there was a heavy fragrance of flowers and lemons, oranges, paw-paw, and kola nuts among many others. More than a tiny cloud of yellow and black butterflies circled around the huge kola nut tree, and then roared up into infinite quiet atmosphere. Yet, the whirring of insects, and constant bleating of goats, broke the silence in the village. Chokah and the other village lads made catapults from small fork-like branches of a gigantic tree that stood there.

Tamba Kolloh had just climbed the tree and picked some fresh kola nuts. He ate some, and tied some in a small bundle for Kumba's mother, Kpannah Mongor. Chokah, his most dynamic emissary, had already left and gone in search of mangoes, paw-paw, guava and other edible berries in the bushes near the village. He was a wild little boy but respected his elders. They gave him incentives to encourage him. He continued his job with ease and joy, and took pleasure in his missions, and was never afraid to enter in homes in the village.

Kumba Mongor surged from behind the woods. She completely surprised Tamba Kolloh. He turned abruptly and smiled softly.

"Why did you send Chokah to call me early in the morning?" she queried softly.

"Kumba, I only wanted to apologize for any inconvenience I might have caused this morning by meeting your mother without your consent," he said with a smiling countenance.

She smiled gently as she paused to sit down on a dry branch of a fallen tree and looked at him curiously and directly in the face, shaking her head gently with a cheerful grin.

"Why did you hurt me last night?" she questioned him boldly.

"I am very sorry and you have to forgive me, Kumba," he said begging her for a sincere forgiveness.

"But you said that you love me, right?" she asked.

"Sincerely my dear, it's no joke, and I will marry you too," he said looking at her with an absolute radiance of pride and love.

Kumba looked at his eyes piteously, and sat down with happiness when she heard, *I will marry you*, in his words. It was exactly what her mother wanted to hear from his mouth. She now felt relieved and could now easily convince her mother that he was indeed the right one for her. She bowed her head in a pensive mood. Tamba Kolloh stood gallantly beside her. They were both lost in what they had proposed to be in the future—husband and wife.

Suddenly, there was a sound somewhere near them. It was indefinable and inexplicable—it sounded louder and louder. Then it stopped and a tortuous silence set in. The eerie spine-chilling atmosphere of the surrounding air numbed their thinking with a sense of hopelessness. Kumba stood very stiff and her face wore an expression of exquisite pearly calm.

Tamba Kolloh took his machete in a lordly gesture. For the first time in her presence, a flicker of devilishness showed in his eyes, and then disappeared as quickly it had come. He had wanted to demonstrate to her that he was very audacious and could attack and kill a lion just to save her in any circumstances. Yet, their hearts were thumping, ears pounding, palms perspiring, and knees shaking. They stood speechless, and each looked with an apprehensive countenance to where they had heard that awful noise.

"What was that?" Tamba said with a growing impatient urgency in his voice.

He decided to go and see what had caused the sibilant whistling and unpleasant noise behind the kola nut tree. A cool wind blew in the surrounding trees, and they felt chilly and very cold. The lovers suspected that some very strange thing was surely going to happen. They allowed the silence to ripen a bit.

Then, within a twinkle of an eye, someone coughed and

gave a loud, abrupt laugh. At the same time, amid smoke, flame, and fumes of noxious gases, Tamba Kolloh shook with a very heavy and a tremulous breath and relaxed slightly. The dizzying sweetness of orange blossoms assaulted their senses. Kumba Mongor then sat sadly with her left hand to her mouth. She was so frightened that she began to gnaw on her thumbnail.

Tamba Kolloh stood silently and waved his left hand to her, urging her to come quickly to him. By the time he had waved twice, urging her to come to see such a very strange sight, he heard a mysterious voice that seemed to be an incantation, commanding him thus:

"Tamba Kolloh, today, you have been chosen not only to be Kumba's husband, but a chief priest, a gifted herbalist, and a witch-hunter, who will perform miracles which no one could elucidate in your day. You have heard that, the symptoms of illness have overpowered me, and even our most powerful *Piomdo (god of good health)* shrine in Fodedu village couldn't cure me. Yet, today, I shall remain the guiding spirit of your race. At any time you want to perform such miracles, come to talk to me under this huge kola nut tree. Playing a flute or a harp, I will make you sing a melodious song. All spiritual powers and mysterious incantations have been transferred into you. You will continue to see more wonders after today in all your dreams. I am old man Nyuma Mongor. Please keep this a secret and marry my daughter Kumba Mongor. Goodbye."

The ghost disappeared.

Tamba Kolloh took a deep breath. He then turned to Kumba and saw her break down in a wail of despair, and he cried incessantly.

"Before I came to join you in the bush, I had a dream in which I saw my father die. In fact, it coincided with Chokah waking me up in the hut," she cried pathetically.

Her voice dwindled significantly. Tamba consoled her as she fell silent and sat gently on the same branch.

"Oh! *Keke*nu (Oh! my father). Oh! *Keke*nu," she repeated the same over and over as she continued to cry.

Tamba laid her in his mighty arms, still perplexed by everything that had taken place. He questioned her softly in a splendid mood.

"Did you see the horrifying event that took place behind the kola nut tree?" he asked.

Kumba sat down timidly and shook her head gently as they both sat on the same branch for a while. Tamba again took her in the crook of his arms as she continued to sob relentlessly.

The sad news of the death of old man Nyuma Mongor spread like wild fire burning in a very dry harmattan bush. Immediately, the sad news was echoed in the Toli Clan, the priests and priestesses, psychics, herbalists, and even other venerable old men and women in the clan; painted their faces with a white chalk made from soft clay excavated from the swamp. They then began a long chanting of sacred verses as a degree of great respect for the dead.

So it was done in those days. The village showed absolute love as they engaged in performing the rites and the appropriate rituals when a chief, a high priest, a warrior, or any venerable man died in the clan.

The late Nyuma Mongor died in Fodedu village. The

corpse was to be transported to Yilandu village. All other arrangements were now underway. The strong men in the village commenced the digging of the grave. Cows and other domestic animals were collected and were slaughtered. Traditional musical stars, comedians, *Bolah* (distant relatives), and important men and women started pouring into the village. The most trusted warriors and hunters continued the blasts from the canons unabated with an endless supply of gunpowder.

Kumba Mongor had already joined the first row of mourners: other family members, and especially those who came from the adjacent villages. They had admired her late father's knowledge and great works as a chief priest in their clan. He had performed with such excellence and had recited some mysterious incantations extremely difficult for any other person to elucidate. They never knew that he had left such a gift and might, with his now son-in-law. Tamba Kolloh, who it was believed, would continue wiping the tears of the idols in the clan for many years.

The late Nyuma Mongor was renowned far and wide. He in fact conjured rings and manufactured amulets, which were worn by most of his kinsmen. Such idols have immense power and provide good luck in the pursuit of life's endless needs. He also revived and helped babies to recuperate after they have been bewitched or over shadowed by the wicked and mysterious claws of the witches and other voodoo men. Nyuma Mongor was also remembered to have prevented any calamity that might have engulfed any village, or the entire Toli clan, by his mysterious deeds. He helped his people to be blessed with bountiful harvests annually and also cured the most deadly *nyangafoo (powdered anthrax),* which was thrown mysteriously on someone by an enemy, even if the person was not present. It made someone's skin itch considerably. It also caused painful spasms. It was the worst curse someone could inflict on any one even to this day in the Kissi land.

He made it possible for someone to fall in love with the mother of the deadliest and the most evil of all land and sea denizens, Mammy Water. He could perform very strange miracles, which made him the giant of the underground world. Now in his place was an energetic young man whose might was greater than anyone in the Toli clan.

Gbekah Kondoh, the chief of Yilandu, and one of the most famous warriors summoned all the elders in the Toli Clan, and even those beyond. He has sent messages by the sound of the *Tambaah* (a traditional drum), which was neatly placed on a high stand built with sticks. Zakah, the most gifted drummer, who knew the differences between the various sonorous beats of that heavy drum, was sent to play so that the other distant villages could know exactly what was taking place in Yilandu.

When the chief sent an emissary, that person was supposed to be a hunter, since people feared to roam the countryside due to reports of attacks by wild animals all over the clan, and even from distant clans like, Bomassadu, Konio, Lelah, and Kundu.

By then, a great cloak of sadness had fallen in the village and the decibels of noise competed with the degree of heat. At the gravesite, massive digging went on. Nyuma Mongor had died in Fodedu, just a distance of two miles from

Yilandu.

The Kissi had a mysterious way of transporting the dead from one village to another, which the tribe accomplished perfectly even without the corpses of those who had died long time ago. In such cases, the rites were performed and libation was poured. A white object, like a coin, a cloth, etc. was blessed by the priests and priestesses, often called *Sokoah (Kissi philosophers).* They didn't unearth the grave to take the decomposed corpse. They instead placed the white object on the grave, and recited a mysterious incantation over and over. They then poured a special ointment in a calabash, and with a few pieces of white and red kola nuts, they blessed the object, which was placed on a youth's head.

They continued in a long procession towards the village where the deceased was to be taken and reburied. The youth who took the object on his head fasted from talking to anyone until he reached the final destination. The long procession involved men and women, hunters, priests and priestesses, children, dogs, other domestic animals. Everything was also done with the intermittent sounds of the native guns, which the tribe's most trusted hunters blasted.

When they had reached the destination, more ceremonies were performed, and the white object was then placed in a wooden plate, and libation was also poured with a long incantation, and buried in a particular spot. More blasts were heard from the guns. Domestic animals like cows, goats, sheep, and fowls were slaughtered to mark the important occasion. Of all the tribes only the Kissi are known to transfer the dead from one village to another, that way. Other villages joined the celebrations that sometimes lasted for days.

The late Nyuma Mongor's case wasn't like that. His corpse was taken to Yilandu since the distance wasn't that far. The mourners had already arrived in Fodedu from all over the Toli and even parts beyond. There was a very large gathering of elders, musical stars, comedians, priests, griots, and chief priests who headed other sacred idols in the entire Kissi land.

In a state burial, the body was to be kept in the chief's decision-making shed. The corpse lay covered neatly in a newly woven country cloth in a perfect condition. Hundreds of mourners sat beside it, their faces pictured great sorrow, as clouds of tears continued to brim in their red eyes. Silence was observed instinctively as the priests recited special mysterious incantations to the Almighty God, and to their forebears who had died and gone long ago. After the recitation of each verse, the huge congregation answered, "Ameeee-nah!"

Tamba Kolloh was among the most versatile and energetic young men who had volunteered to transport the corpse to Yilandu. He hadn't started to play his wonders yet, and so in Fodedu, he was a spectator. His face had gone wintry as long as Kumba Mongor had been shedding tears. Yet, he was looked upon as a very promising young man, and stood with a dignified pose, as he was now confident that he was surely going to become a very powerful chief priest in Toli. From the gesticulations of the elders in the chief's shed, it appeared that they seemed to be arguing over the most appropriate way of transporting the corpse.

The traditional singers played their drums. The *griots* were ready as well. The most dynamic female shakers players, like Sia Ngeleh-*Queseo FORYOH,* gathered, among the many others. They sang eulogies in the form of ballads, dirges, epics, and satires. Each group sang and eulogized their heroes, living or dead. They called the names of mighty men like Chief *Gbekah Kondo*, who was always praised as a powerful warrior, and nation builder.

Another, Chief Holloh, was also renowned for his mystic powers—when he called out loudly the name of anyone, that person was forced to attend to nature, like to urinate or defecate on his behalf. He conjured amulets, rings and other exotic herbs with which he cured strange sickness. He was also a witch doctor. Yet, *Gbekah Kondo* was the most feared all over Kissi land.

These were wonderful men, who lived and were respected during their lifetimes. They forever lived in the minds of their people. The knowledge they shared with them was based on ancient traditions never proven by the touchstones of our time. The late Nyuma Mongor was the last spiritually gifted person to live in the clan. He had already chosen Tamba Kolloh to continue in his footsteps. The shrines and oracles were only visited under the protection of the priests and priestesses. They performed the ceremonies there, and with the vacuum created by Nyuma Mongor's death, Tamba Kolloh was surely going to revive the tradition and wipe the tears of the idols in Kissi land for many years.

CHAPTER TWO

The sun rose high in the sky, and Fodedu was now very congested. When the time came for the procession to take Nyuma Mongor's corpse to its destination, an old woman and priestess called *Kolooh* had tied mysterious beads of different colors around her neck, which were also tied around the waists of some other women. She had white paint on her face, her breasts were naked, and she prayed that the Almighty God may bless the footpath against poisonous snakes, scorpions, and other deadly insects or voodoo men who might keep them from going. She had a mysterious tail in her right hand, and a small calabash into which she poured a small quantity of an exotic black liquid, and put the tail into the calabash, sprinkling the contents all over the village, as far as to the footpath to dispel evil spirits away.

Kolooh was also believed to have been a deity and had almost the same supernatural powers as Nyuma Mongor. After she had sprinkled for over an hour, the entire crowd became calm and quiet. One could have dropped a pin, and heard it fall loudly. She then ran to a distant baobab tree and disappeared behind it, pouring the liquid on the roots of the tree and singing a mysterious dirge. It appeared as if she were asking an idol for permission for the long procession to pass through. There she poured some libation too.

In the chief's shed, she ran and prostrated herself beside the corpse. She then mumbled a long and involved incantation and whispered into the ears of the corpse. It was indeed a blood-chilling sight to see, and it ignited a quiver of fear in the hearts of the onlookers. The little children cried and were comforted in their mother's arms. *Kolooh* still swam about relentlessly as if trying to find the most appropriate means of leaving Fodedu village. She held her ground indignantly. Some spectators, who knew what she was doing, chortled at the entire episode and encouraged her never to relent from fighting those evil forces. She was indeed a great fighter.

Dark clouds gathered and promised a downpour of rain. There were few droplets, but *Kolooh*, popularly called Heiningbeh (lie calmly), narrated a special incantation and boasted that it was only going to rain on her back, but not in Fodedu that day, until the entire burial ceremony was performed. No one knew how the Kissi people got such mystic powers. They narrated a long incantation, and at the same time calling God Almighty to answer them. It actually worked. They could stop a downpour of rain. *Kolooh* continued to regale them on the mysteries her performance divulged. She was now the only actress on the stage and the entire village was silent, and looked up to her for deliverance.

She sweated profusely from the running and at a specific point in her ceremony, she disclosed, "the gods of our forefathers have agreed for the dead to leave Fodedu to Yilandu."

There was great relief and happiness as the crowd that had gathered bantered and thundered with enthusiasm and praises for her.

"No one should stand in front of the corpse. Adults

should lead the way and mothers and fathers are advised to protect their children. No woman should tie a head tie, and the pallbearers should be barefooted," she yelled this warning with very stern eyes.

At the end of her speech, there were four blasts from the cannons. The hunters had gathered enough gunpowder, and were ready to shoot. Chief Nyuma Fodedu had been more circumspect, more humble and pleased, because the visitors had respected and strictly adhered to their culture and custom. He then presented a calabash full of kola nuts and praised *Kolooh* as he gathered the large propellers of his huge country cloth gown, and stood with dignity. He also presented a white cock, a sack of rice husk rice, and thanked Heiningbeh for the interesting spiritual education she had given them on the appropriate norms that fit the burial of such a chief priest in their clan.

With all the gifts, they anticipated the huge reception that awaited them in Yilandu. There, they were to perform more miracles before the final ceremony. The elders had already gathered and hung their heads, and they waved for the procession to go.

The village singers, chiefs, and elders led the way behind the pallbearers. Heiningbeh stood in front of the chiefs, although she ran ahead of them on the footpath at intervals, and returned hastily singing a very melodious song and shaking the mysterious tail in her right hand. The singers sang songs of love, of ancient traditions and customs, and also of their heroes and their greatest deeds in the clan: endurance, humor, and benevolence. Nyuma Mongor was considered a hero, and one of the greatest men that even lived in their clan. The chiefs were praised as well.

Praising the chiefs was the duty of *Yamba* Yilandu, the greatest *griot* in Yilandu. He was an old man whose praises in very short and witty songs never offered vague and nebulous, assertions. He sang clear, reasonable, convincing and moral explanations of any mysteries he wanted to divulge. In his witty songs, he used to ask his admirers, "What does time and human life mean in our infinite and limitless world, governed by pride and ignorance?"

He felt that it wasn't necessary for man to keep up a semblance of dignity but to assume an air of mystery in propagating knowledge being transmitted to the younger generation. He often smiled and loved to sing such eulogies with handsome predictions; and he was loved by the children, and he shared fun with them.

Tamba Kolloh was among the pallbearers. He marched with dignity and with an inflexible firmness of purpose. *Yamba* caught sight of him in the procession and yelled out his name, "You are going to be a powerful chief priest in Yilandu—Tamba!"

Also among the pallbearers was Tengbeh, who was renowned for fighting the baboons on the Ngebadu Hill; there was Veeseebendu (mighty animal), who was accused of indulging into the practice of cannibalism in the distant parts of the clan. There were lots of other very powerful men, who were all pallbearers on that very famous day.

Yamba called all of them - comrades of valor, stamina and intelligence, and said that Tamba Kolloh was going to be their head. There was joy and fear in the very long procession of mourners. Their eyes welled with clouds of tears, and women wiped the profuse sweat from their bodies, and the bodies of their loved ones with their head ties.

Yamba Yilandu again yelled out a very short and witty eulogy that ended in the following expression: "Oh! Tamba Kolloh, boldness sometimes brings its own rewards. Oh!" *Yamba* continued. "Oh! These lions of the Toli! Oh! These illustrious men with supernatural powers." He died down calmly as if he hadn't said anything.

Yamba then put his right hand in the huge pockets of country cloth gown, and took a few sips of the *Tamba Nanjahn* gin, (cane juice). He also sniffed a few tips of his neatly pounded tobacco and shook his head accordingly. Seemingly, the rising sun greeted them with a dazzling brilliance, and he laughed good-naturedly at them all. He played a small shaker, which he shook, and the colored beads around it produced a check-check sound. It was the only musical instrument he carried with him. He stepped heavily on his right leg, his deformity since childhood. He sweated profusely as he embarked on the long and arduous march with the mourners.

The drummers and the other female shakers players continued singing intermittent verses, "Oh! *Kolooh*! You have helped the success of this day."

"For the sun is now shining very brilliantly in the azure sky," echoed *Yamba.*

The journey was spirited and the ambience very lively. All the mourners marched steadily. They sang and joked with one another in harmonious propositions. Some suggested that life was a jest shown by all things. The Kissi believed that everything was transient in existence. Yet, they all continued to lament for the dead. They also believed that death was just the reincarnation of the soul, and that although Nyuma Mongor was dead, yet he lived among them.

The golden silence of the midday sun predicted that the mourners were awaited urgently in Yilandu. They had traveled over the few hours sluggishly, and were now not too far from their destination. The forest became eerie. The procession could now hear the chirping of the birds. There was a very loud cry of the toucan—it signified something, only *Kolooh* could decipher it. They also heard a large whirring of countless insects. Monkeys danced on the branches of the tall trees above them. The matchless caress of the forest breeze anticipated the wonders of what was going to be portrayed in the rituals in the village.

There was a smiling gentleness in the Kissi culture, a liveliness of manner and the oldest tradition of elegance and beauty. As the Jawee Mountain looked at them in far the distance, on the horizon, they could see lofty lookouts and intricate blooms and legends and lore that sing of the might of the Kissi. It also gave the people plenty to talk about.

A viper swiftly crossed the footpath ahead of the pallbearers. Nyuma Mongor's corpse was carried lying on their heads on stretcher made of sticks, which the pallbearers transported comfortably. Tamba Kolloh was the only one who saw the reptile. It predicted the presence of the Nyuma Mongor's ghost ahead of them. He nodded complacently, as the procession was now nearing the bushes on the outskirts of Yilandu.

But from where they stood, they could see that the village was in a great turmoil. There was crying all over. It appeared as if a fresh genocide had taken place in the village, and that the survivors mourned the dead. Some of the cries resembled the wails of the living, or the shrieks of the wounded that lay, dying.

The distant noises echoed all kinds of lamentation. The people of Yilandu cried for someone who was once a savior of their village and clan. The entire clan was represented in that procession. Lots of others started taking other footpaths to enter into the village through the coffee and cacao plantations that surrounded the village. The pallbearers and the other elders waited for directives from *Kolooh* before they could enter into the village. Some stood in a stiff position, and she awaited a special command from the gods before they could enter into Yilandu. The mourners stood at the crossroads. They could clearly see the village. In the setting sun, the voices of the mourners filled the air.

Kolooh then ran into the village and poured some of the strange black liquid into the grave, and ran again toward the procession. She also narrated a mysterious incantation. They could see flecks dancing in her black brown eyes. Her cheeks were rosy and she looked around beseechingly. She was indeed a woman renowned for her spiritual power. A huge crowd converged on her in the village, but she never uttered a word to anyone. She swiftly returned to the crossroads to signal the pallbearers and the entire procession to enter into the village by shaking the tail in her right hand in the air in a jerking and dancing mood.

The experience was horrific, imaginative and suspenseful. The little children felt a thrill of fear. The babies clung to their mothers' backs, while others clung to their arms. They all looked astounded. Yet, their eyes brimmed with a cloud of tears. The hunters soon united, and gave some huge blasts from the heavy guns, which they had loaded with more than enough gunpowder.

Chief *Gbekah Kondo* welcomed the mourners and treated them with the respect bequeathed by traditional custom, with a special veneration.

Kola nuts were shared, and fresh water was given to the strong men who had perfectly laid the corpse at state in Chief *Gbekah Kondo*'s decision-making shed. Food was shared according to status and personality. The mourners ate with their bare hands from wooden plates, clay pots, and even from iron pots (the people already had iron and they manufactured iron pots, knives and spoons).

The old dashed a few grains of cooked rice on the floor. They also poured the *Tamba Nanjahn gin (cane juice)* on the ground in the form of a libation, as they invited the dead to come join them, to eat and be merry. Others threw a few grains of cooked food near the corpse. Yet, the lamentation continued unabated.

Kumba Mongor was among the family members and other relatives and friends who had tied their head ties around their waists. They had also loosed their hair and had fallen several times on the dirty and muddy ground, crying incessantly, which showed ardent love, and lament for the dead. It also showed an image of cultural respectability.

Earlier, Kumba had stood on the main footpath that led

into the village. She had stood among her peers and other relatives to witness and to honor the entering of the corpse of her late father into the village. She glanced at Tamba Kolloh who was the head pallbearer. They had taken the corpse in groups four men at a time. Everyone could hear Kumba Mongor crying at the outskirts of the village.

"Oh! *Keke*nu. (Oh! My father.) Oh! *Keke*nu. *Keke*, loh que nan chaya-ning? (Dad, when shall we see again?)" She cried continuously. "May God be with you *Keke!*"

Immediately, Tamba Kolloh spotted her and marched majestically to show her, courage, love, endurance and benevolence. Tamba sympathized deeply for the Mongor family, and he wished to win her love. He looked sideways, and they glanced at each other. Kumba nodded in response, as if urging him to endure the weight of her late father's heavy corpse that lay comfortably on his head, with great pride and dignity. The young women who stood closer to her watched the scene with rapturous pride.

"Um-humm, this is one of signs of the greatest love adventure ever seen in our village," disclosed Sia Focko with a twitch of smile.

"Uh, you mean the friendship that had developed between Kumba Mongor and Tamba Kolloh?" questioned Tewa Sakillah.

"Um-Humm, Tewa. You can see how he was sweating under the corpse, and marched energetically just to show that his love is the greatest. Even their parents have already grown accustomed to their friendship, which has grown very wild in the village," Sia Focko whispered scornfully to Tewa. "I once saw her coming from Tamba Kolloh's room very early in the morning; and she lied to her mother that she had slept in her grandfather's hut."

"Eh! Eh! Eh! Sia, you mean Kumba Mongor has already known man-business?" said Tewa.

"Of course," she replied grimly. "Wait, Tewa. Do you think that she is still a little girl?"

They both gurgled with laughter.

"You can now see how fatuously proud she has been over the last months. She has grown very wild, although more charming and with long tender legs. Her pubic hair has bulged and her voice has taken frightening dimensions," said Sia Focko. "Above all, she succumbed to rudeness with fearlessness in her behavior. We have all seen her actions these days as a tangible proof of her ineffable romantic adventure," Sia concluded with a derisive laughter.

Yet in the village, final burial preparations were going on as they tried to finish the very long and tedious ritual that was most appropriate for a burial of a chief priest in their culture. It was done amid lamentation, fun and grief. The *Bolah,* a very powerful band of members of one's family or distant relatives of the deceased, came and danced, and made the occasion to look more interesting with great fun, laughter, mischief and modest courage.

The distant mourning relatives trivialized any grievances that had previously existed in families and in the clan with imitations of past and present happenings, and with profound and boundless love, fun and mischief. They had the entire occasion under their control. Some of them didn't engage in the crying and sorrow as the culture was portrayed. They even abused the village chief and caused mild violence that resulted in loud, unnecessary noises, without anyone bothering them because they were the *Bolah.*

They even pretended to seize the corpse and demanded a handsome ransom of abundant quality without petulance. According to the norms of the Kissi culture, they halted all burial ceremonies until the request of the *Bolah* was fulfilled. Such ransom comes in the form of a cow, a goat, a bushel of husked or cleaned rice, or a tin of palm oil. They made the occasion very joyous by even requesting domestic animals like, a cat, a dog, or a cock, etc.

Kendema was the spokesman, and most powerful head of the *Bolah,* and of the Mongor family. They encircled the corpse as if it were a prisoner of war whose freedom was only to be granted after meeting certain demands.

Old man Kendema was renowned and feared through the entire clan for his bravery and his tactical genius in settling ancient feuds and ethnic vendettas. He was also one of those who prevented any kind of misfortune in their clan by placating the gods at the oracles and shrines of the clan. The elders of the Mongor family had an urgent meeting to challenge their impetuous *Bolah* on that day.

Tamba Kolloh had perfectly played the role of a son-in-law, and he gradually realized that he had already attained a certain measure of fame in Yilandu, the clan, and in the Mongor family. He was invited by them and honored to be the spokesperson of the family. They thought he was the most competent to challenge their very noisy and pertinacious *Bolah*, so that they could have stopped the niggardly bargaining of the dead with such astuteness. By a special dispensation from all families involved, Tamba Kolloh was to play the role of an important family man in the village that day.

The drummers and *griots* continued their activities as mourners from the distant villages continued to pour into Yilandu. Tamba Kolloh surged forward. All the people looked at him for the first time with a courteous expression. It was after challenging the *Bolah* that he was given the opportunity to assert the dignity of his position in the illustrious Mongor family. He waved both hands manfully in the air. All the drummers, *griots*, and dancers who had had a sleepless night and grown haggard from drinking the locally manufactured *Tamba Nanjahn gin*, brawled among themselves.

It was very difficult to obtain complete quietness. Yet, when the chance was finally given to him to speak, Tamba Kolloh surged forward. *Yamba* echoed some hints of praises for him.

"Ouh! Ouh! Ouh!" said *Yamba* as he sat beside the few kegs of palm wine. "La-mae-yoooh! (Silence)," he again shouted, and performed his duty ably, conscientiously and neatly. "Ouh!" he continued. "One of your most versatile, eloquent, dynamic, and prominent sons, Tamba Kolloh, wants to speak to all of you who have gathered here today."

There was still some comic and gleeful chattering on corners.

"Ouh! Ouh! Ouh!" he shouted for the last time and the demand for silence was observed.

There was still some brawling by those completely intoxicated men in distant comers of the village. The children joked with the drunken men who had slept outdoors, and brawled. Yet, others were amazed and stood speechless to listen to what Tamba was going to say to all of them.

Tamba Kolloh never knew that it was that particular speech on that day that was going to crown all his future activities in the Toli Clan. He then cleared his throat and shouted, "May the soul of our father rest in peace in the arms of our forefathers who have also died and long gone to God Almighty."

"Ameeeeee-nah!" the large crown of mourners responded as the decibels of mourning competed with the degrees of heat.

Kumba Mongor had cried for long hours now. She sat tiredly on a wooden stool and nodded her head to what was said that day. Then, she noticed an elderly woman, also a mourner who had come from a distant village to attend her father's funeral, standing beside her. She rose and gave her the wooden stool to sit while she stood instead. Such was politely done according to their culture. The young gave seats to the old.

"Ah! Tamba Kolloh, he is a man among men, for even a toad can't run for nothing in the day- something must be chasing it." *Yamba* shouted and cooled down in his melodious and very soft voice.

Tamba Kolloh continued, "Thoughts can never become lived until they are clothed with very deep feelings. I would first of all like to thank all of you for leaving your distant villages—and especially now when the palm birds are eating the rice on our farms—to come to help us bury our father, the late Nyuma Mongor. I would also like to extend my sincerest thanks to Chief *Gbekah Kondo* and the other venerable elders for the ebullient success so far. I was selected by the Mongor family to present these gifts to our most honorable, trusted, but good-for-nothing *Bolah*. The entire crowd burst with great laughter."

"Le*Ndeh* gbaei! Gbaei! (it is the truth), *Bolah* are just a good-for-nothing bunch of stupid people," echoed *Yamba*, as he tried to shout to those who stood in the distant parts of the village.

The drunken men, who were teased by the children around them, shouted exactly what *Yamba* had said, and the laughter continued unabated. The *Bolah* too retaliated by telling the large crowd of mourners that they were all monkeys, and stupid fools. This was how they conducted burial ceremonies with great fun and mischief. Some cried as others joked in comers. Yet, they were all there for a specific purpose: to bury the dead, and to fulfill the appropriate norms that were required during the grieving period.

Tamba Kolloh then produced a basket filled with the dry leaves and dirt, which he presented to the *Bolah* as payment for the ransom they had requested earlier. An immense roar of laughter broke the hushed silence from the huge crowd of mourners that had gathered as they all joked around with each other. According to the ancient norms, anything that was presented to the *Bolah* was to be accepted. It was just a way of sharing jokes and fun and to keep the idols alive.

Tamba Kolloh continued, "In that respect, I would like to present to the *Bolah* a cow, a goat, and the other things that were previously requested by them."

For a cow, a dog was presented. For a goat, a cat was presented. For the sack of husked rice, a big basin of cooked rice was presented along with a calabash of kola nuts, and sweet rice bread, which was made by soaking cleaned rice in a calabash and pounding it inside a mortar with a pestle; it was prepared during all sacred occasions and also given to the dead at the oracles and shrines.

After the historic donation, the people of Yilandu told their *Bolah* that they had come to beg for food in their village since they were starving to death in their homes. *Yamba* then put his hand inside his pocket and took out his small bottle. He drank from it, and presented the rest of the *Tamba Nanjahn* gin to the *Bolah*. The mourners couldn't wait to burst with derisive laughter again. Food and drinks like the palm and bamboo wine, and the *Tamba Nanjahn* were distributed. Everything was done, under the supervision of the elders.

The dancers enjoyed the food in specific social groups. The griots were often in the company of the chiefs, as they benefited from any donations that were presented to them in the village chief's hut. They ate, chatted, danced in the afternoon, and in the evening—as the corpse was to sleep one night, and be buried the next day.

The Kissi never embalmed the dead. They believed that life was just a continuing process, and death was just like sleeping to them. The gravesite was located in the compound of the deceased. It was for him to remain as a guiding spirit of the family even after death. The men who played the talking drums sang rap music. Nyuma Mongor, in his day, loved them. They sang ballads, epics, and dirges. There was no sleeping in the evening. The mourners danced the whole night.

The sun was rising very fast the next day. The mourners were rushing to the gravesite to fulfill the final burial ceremony. When all the wives and children, together with the extended family of the deceased and the *Bolah* had gathered, Njopoei, an old man, and also considered one of the most gifted in performing burial rites, came forward to perform the final rituals of the burial ceremony. He stood tall and erect with the aid of a cane, and gathered the huge arms of his country cloth gown and said, "As we all deeply grieve the death of one of our most prominent chief priests in our clan, we should also pray to God Almighty for his soul to rest in peace. Nyuma Mongor was a father, a savior, a kind man, and a competent herbalist, and chief priest. His works were so admirable that no one will be able to take his place for a long time."

Yamba the griot shouted every word that came from Njopoei's mouth. Those are the good qualities of a professional village griot even to this day, among the Kissi. Many of the griots sat on mats, others on wooden benches, while still others stood. The singers sang in low tunes as the rites were performed. A cool breeze blew around the gravesite and *Kolooh* came forward with such a modest courage and smiled with exhilaration and with the emotion of victory. It was an eerie expression, as if she conversed with the dead. She lifted her mysterious tail and declared:

"There is glory, rewards, and recognition for all the time he spent in our clan. The activities have been spirited and

Nyuma Mongor has reached his destination to the home of the dead."

She held the calabash on her head tightly with her left hand and sprinkled the black liquid with the tail in her right hand in all directions in the village. She also visited the gravesite, and sprinkled the liquid into it. It was to dispel the evil spirits and to open the door for the dead to travel to the home of the dead in peace.

There was a renewed crying in all quarters of Yilandu. Kpannah Mongor, the head wife of the deceased and Kumba's mother, was held several times in her relatives' arms, for she continued to cry as if in an anguish of great pain. Her children and those of her mate, Finda Mongor, cried bitterly to demonstrate that the affection was genuine and the loss of their father was very severe to all of them. As for the *Bolah* they continued to regale the people with unending acts and scenes with antics that created much fun and mischief.

Immediately the noises died down, Njopoei continued: "Today, Nyuma Mongor is gone, but his deeds will be always remembered from generation to generation in Toli. They will always remain with us."

"Ouh! Ouh!" *Yamba* shouted again as he urged the mourners to listen to what the old man had to say.

Njopoei continued, "He lived his life perfectly. He demonstrated his love for all of us abundantly, and has taught us some knowledge based on our ancient tradition now to be proven by the touchstone of our time. He was a perfect leader whose teachings connected us with the fundamentals of our ancient history, our norms, and traditions that blessed our pantheons. He divulged those beliefs and ancient practices at out oracles and shrines, which were lost in the midst of time. Ah! Nyuma Mongor."

His voice quivered as his eyes brimmed with a cloud of tears. He took a deep, tremulous breath, relaxed slightly and again continued:

"Nyuma Mongor, prepare ahead of us, for we shall meet one day. Please extend our heartfelt messages to those who have died ahead of you and may your soul rest in peace," he sorrowfully concluded. "Nyuma Mongor, please greet my grandmother Mama Nya*Ndeh* in the land of the dead," a drunken mourners shouted from a remote part of the village. It ignited some laughter in the village too.

"Ah! In this world of ours, everything is transient in existence, "*Yamba* echoed.

Some elders had met in the chief's shed, and were murmuring sacred incantations to the oracles and the shrines of the clan. The traditional singers and drummers played continuously. *Queseo* Sia Ngeleh *FORYOH*, one of the most prolific female shaker players, had commenced playing, and gathered some fresh spectators, as well as those who brawled and slept drunk overnight.

Tamba Kolloh and a group of men came forward and descended into the grave. They were directed to spread the newly woven country cloth donated by Tadanpoli to the Mongor family, in it. Also, in the grave, were neatly placed boxes of the things that were previously used by the deceased on earth. They were his clothes, his machetes and knives, a pipe, gunpowder, some very strange shells, and much more. The things were neatly placed in boxes, and put in the corners of the grave.

It was believed that, in the ancient time in Kissi land, when such very prominent men, women, and chiefs, died domestic slaves and horses, were also killed and buried along with their masters to accompany them.

Yet, as their idols continued to shed their tears over the years, these practices were stopped abruptly. They knew that Nyuma Mongor wouldn't be able to transport all the utensils and the other basic things all by himself to the home of the dead. Some believed that he was going to be assisted by his kinsmen who had died, and waited there to receive him.

Kolooh explained such unearthly episodes to the mourners with a firm and authoritative resonance. She sobbed intermittently, thought, and shook incredibly. She appeared as if she had gone there before, and had returned to tell her kinsmen about the after life experiences. She was also a gifted priestess.

Yamba again signaled for silence at the gravesite, as Njopoei continued with the final burial rites, "The God of the sky, the God of our forefathers, the God of the rivers, mountains, trees, etc."

"Ameee-nah!" The large crowd of mourners answered together.

Njopoei continued, "Help your son Nyuma Mongor to see a clear passage, and to make a successful journey to the home of the dead."

"*Ameee-nah*!" the mourners answered again.

"I would then like to call upon all those the deceased owed in his day to come forward so that the Mongor family could repay them. It should be done with open hearts and with the frankness of purpose so that the deceased may not encounter any challenges as he makes ready to journey to the home of our dead forefathers."

Njopoei paused and, although tears welled in his eyes, yet the mourners approached them with notable consolations, "Yes, I am Sahr Sakillah Kpakah. The late Nyuma Mongor asked me to give him five sacks of husked rice, which he would have repaid after the harvest season. Yet, since God has now taken his life, the Mongor family should use the rice to feed the steady stream of mourners that will continue to pour into the village, to pay condolences, after the burial," he concluded tearfully.

"*Balika*h! *Balika*h! *Balika*h! Sakillah," the mourners said thanking him.

"Ah! Sahr Sakillah, you are a rock in Yilandu," *Yamba* eulogized, and he silenced the crowd again cunningly.

"I am Finda Tambelloh. Nyuma Mongor took ten bottles of *Tamba Nanjahn gin (cane juice)* from me for the laborers, who plowed his huge farm," Finda said, unable to conclude her speech because she was angrily told to sit down, or, go away. She was a trouble-shooter.

Her lips were as red as palm oil, a clear indication of the previous night's drunken spree. She yelled tearfully, and her mouth faded to an outburst of loud crying. Her kinsmen held her; pulled her away annoyingly.

"Ah! Finda, you have put Yilandu and Toli to shame again today," *Yamba* echoed, and there was laughter in most parts of the village. She was considered the most hateful person in the village that day.

"I am Sahr Ponpondo, a blacksmith here in Yilandu. Nyuma Mongor took three matches and five hoes from me when the plowing season commenced in the village. He promised to repay after the farming season with two sacks of the husked rice," he said tears welling in his eyes; he was pulled away gently.

"Ah! Ponpondo, you are one of the lions in Yilandu," *Yamba* again echoed cunningly, while raising his voice and singing a witty chorus in the form of a dirge, as he died down silently.

He was the most gifted of griots. He sang those witty songs in an attempt to keep the silence after the noises of the huge crowd of mourners that had gathered that day, was about to get out of control.

Many of the mourners sat beside each other. Some shook their heads incredibly, while others looked up in the sky. All was perfectly under control, as the success was now seen in the way they had handled their traditional norms and values. Although in general, it isn't a good idea to demand anything from the dead—if a demand were made, it is supposed to be fulfilled according to their custom. They also believed that fulfilling a demand allowed the soul to rest in peace.

The sun was now standing in the sky, and those who were not standing under the eaves of the mud huts or under the shades of the cacao and coffee trees sweated profusely from the heat of the tropical sun. Yet, all attendants enjoyed the ceremony and bore the hot rays of the sun with hardened courage, and comfort.

In a corner of the village, a drunken old man sat sadly

and held his chin with the palm of his left hand. He smiled slightly and questioned himself, "Why did Finda Tambelloh tell this very large crowd of mourners that Nyuma Mongor took Tamba Nanjah gin from *her*? She shouldn't have said that in the first place. She disgraced the entire village, and the entire Toli Clan. She has given enough gun powder to our *Bolah* to shoot at us in the village," he said with dignity, yet with great annoyance too.

He sat comfortably and watched the entire ceremony at a distance from under the shadow of the trees near the village. There were also some elders who sat beside kegs of palm and bamboo wine; they had tapped earlier that day. Some were already intoxicated from drinking especially the thick bamboo wine; their eyes were already shinning like those of a viper.

Amid the incidents, Tamba Kolloh emerged again, and stepped forward. He cleared his Kola nut infested throat just to get control of his voice, and to assume the power and self-confidence that the Mongor family had invested in him, and declared, "People of the Toli Clan, lend me your ears."

"Ah! Tamba Kolloh, there are men among men; for even an elephant knows its match," *Yamba* echoed to get silence.

Tamba Kolloh continued, "I stand before you with the respect of our great Chief *Gbekah Kondo*, and all the elders to mourn a father, a wonderful kinsman, an uncle and, above all, one who gave life to most of us today."

"Ah! Tamba Kolloh, another powerful chief priest is already in the making in Yilandu and Toli," *Yamba* echoed, and silence was observed again.

Tamba Kolloh continued, "I represent the Mongor family here today, and they have asked me to greet all of you. Death indeed is an end to everything, but not an end to our unity, our pride and our culture as great people. I would then like to humbly request for the presence of all those who have voiced openly that the deceased owed them in the chiefs shed for a brief meeting," he concluded with an authoritative resonance in his manly voice.

As *Yamba* continued to laud his name and fame, Tamba Kolloh was now realizing that he was indeed becoming a great herbalist and respected man in Yilandu, and beyond.

"Oh! Tamba Kolloh, a warrior's knife is never hidden from his enemies," *Yamba* yelled again, and silence was recognized.

He spotted Chief *Gbekah Kondo* who was also called Kondo Gbekah. He was indeed a very powerful chief and a warrior in his day.

"Ouh! Ouh! Ouh!" said the griot. "The mighty Chief *Gbekah Kondo* is on his legs."

Yamba again urged his kinsmen to listen to such an important warrior among them. The chief thanked all the mourners and then recited an eerie incantation.

Each verse ended with a long "*Ameee-nah*!" from the crowd.

He then ordered the men to lay the corpse inside the grave, as the sun was now falling towards the eastern horizon. It was the duty of a warrior to make such a command in those circumstances. The wives of the deceased together with their children came forward to bid their final farewell. The children were told to throw some handfuls of dirt inside the grave.

Kolooh was then given the chance to perform the final burial rites. The elders stood and stretched their hands forward and they recited the dirge of the dead. There was crying all over, followed by lots of farewells—no smiles. The occasion became solemn and more fearful for the little children. The drummers played, and the great singers and dancers challenged the beats of the drums with exquisite styles, and melodious songs.

Queseo Sia Ngeleh *FORYOH* played the shakers, and her small group of backers raised their voices with their mellifluous voices. There was crying and dancing in all the comers of the village. The goats bleated, the cows mooed, and the dogs barked continuously amid the thundering of the drums and the shakers. The men, women, children, old and young, were all traditionally acclimated to the hazards of the sleepless nights over the rituals performed in sacred burials. There they stood and watched in deep silence, while a few patches of yelling continued in the background. The young men continued to shovel mud in the grave.

The music and dancing continued as *Yamba* echoed a few dirges praising the ancient times and love for the deceased. The guns sounded. Mothers again held the hands of their young ones or had their infants clinging to their breasts as they breast-fed them. As the dancing reached its climax in the village, the mourners started leaving the gravesite in smaller and in larger groups. It then continued in twos and threes, until the entire place was completely deserted and remained lonesome. It was dark, eerie and fearful at night. The sky was stitched with stars and the moon permitted the mourners to continue dancing and crying, and all was done with much fun in the village for several days.

Early the next day, the elders paid a visit at the Ngebadu Hill and poured some libation for the dead at a sacred place, where a huge rock perfectly lay on another rock, which may have been caused by some natural forces, a place considered very sacred by the Kissi.

The dancing that followed the next days was uniquely performed. The dancers would reach individual mud huts as the drummers played, while the singers sang tunefully. The elder whose compound they had reached, presented them with gifts like kola nuts, cooked rice, palm or bamboo wine, and *Tamba Nanjah* gin.

The griots headed by *Yamba* accompanied the dancers too. They stood and repeated every word that each elder that was honored said, or on whose compound they had reached. The elder would then dance, and thanked them for visiting his home and family. The young women took head-ties form their heads, and gently waved them on the faces of dancers who were chiefs and deities in the village, and clan.

Although burial was an act of great sorrow, yet, the Kissi danced, and cried at the same time—which demonstrated their ardent love in memory of the deceased, and recognized the family the deceased left behind. It was such activities that brought them together, unifying and solidifying long lasting friendship, and love among them.

CHAPTER THREE

Many of the mourners couldn't partake in the burial ceremony that lasted for days in Yilandu. Early in the morning, they left hurriedly for their farms, and joined the festivities again in the evening. The rice was now ripe on the farms and the harvest season had already approached.

To visit someone on the farms in those days was very dangerous indeed because of the stones that were thrown to far distances on the farms, to drive the noisy palm birds. The farmers stood on high stands built with sticks and threw those stones with their slings, at the same time yelling to scare the birds.

The noisy palm birds and the lovebirds were the most destructive to the rice on the farms—coming only in noisy groups to damage the rice on the farms. Yet, insects and other destructive nocturnal animals enjoyed the rice, cucumber, cassava and other vegetables that grew on the farms as well.

The farmers manufactured slings by cutting palm fronds and peeling the long leaves they wove to make two long ropes. A pocket was made at the tips of the ropes from which a stone was thrown far distances. After the stone throwing, a very sharp noise was heard. It was the stone and the noise that scared those destructive birds. The *fandah (sling)* was manufactured on all the farms.

The farmers also made traditional musical instruments to play on the high stands. One of such they called, *Kaelendon (balafon),* which they manufactured by cutting special short sticks that were peeled and dried in the sun. They were crossed on two short sticks to produce balafon type sounds. The farmers played this instrument on those high stands in both the mild and hot burning sun. So tuneful were they, that even today, one could still hear singers and players of the musical instrument on the high stands of farms, as they echo the lyric, and epics songs of old.

Among the ancient men who portrayed the legends and lore of the natives was Zakah. He built a high stand and, during the bird scaring season and the harvest season, he played the *Kaelendon* and sang with a musical voice that made even the rice harvesters on distant farms nodded their heads.

He also invented sweet songs that matched the tunes. On his farm when the clouds gave way to the rising sun and cleared the sky, he was heard in his most tuneful tenor voice, singing sweet songs. One of such songs that he was most known for was this:

(Kissi Version)
Oh! Sia
Demul-lah me paendu-chor-chor
Oh! Sia
Demul-lah me paendu-chor-chor
Domah nyemani?
Demul-lah me paendu-chor -chor
Kokoh Nyemani?
Demul-lah me paendu-chor-chor
Oh! Sia
Demul-lah me paendu-chor-chor (Repeat)

(English version)
Oh! Sia
Tell me to buy it quick-quick
You want a blouse?
Tell me to buy it quick-quick
You want a head-tie?
Tell me to buy it quick-quick
Oh! Sia (Repeat)

Zakah was renowned for having received a special charm from the late Nyuma Mongor in the form of a ring he wore on his left finger. It made him more handsome, debonair, and gave him an admirable and complaisant attitude so that he was loved by his people. Any time he started playing the *Kaelendon*, other musicians joined in from the distant farms. They copied his tunes, and they sent messages to each other in tunes from those farms.

Even the snakes left the bushes to come to listen under his stand. That was why he preferred to be alone on his stand when he played. Birds that were driven from the other farms came close to listen to such sweet tunes, played so that no human being could neither re-play nor decipher the meanings—because he had a special charm. He was indeed a singer of splendid accomplishment, rare beauty and power.

Kpannah Mongor met Tewa Kolloh, Tamba's mother, on the Kolloh's farm after the burial ceremony. They discussed in detail the growing relationship between Tamba and Kumba. During the conversation Kpannah Mongor thanked Tewa for the bravery shown by her son and the assistance Tamba had given the Mongor family during the burial ceremony of her late husband.

"May his soul rest in peace," the both of them said.

The women shrugged their shoulders and thought of the horror of death as they sat on an old log that lay beside the barn.

"The loveliness of Tamba Kolloh's manner was instinctively acquired through a tradition of hospitality that began when his grandfather," Tewa said with great conviction. "Bandakillie Fugbu died in Yilandu many years ago before he was even born. I have often told him about the death of his great grandfather, and also told him about the immense assistance and hospitality that all our kinsmen showed us during the period of our bereavement. It clearly indicates a smiling gentleness about our culture."

They looked at each other with beaming expressions. Kpannah nodded her head in benediction as they entered into the barn and sat on wooden stools. Tewah gave Kpannah a piece of a white kola nut, which as she broke, and made a sharp noise. She chewed a piece and kept the other piece inside a pocket in her head tie. The person that visited was offered a piece of kola nut according to their custom.

Sitting down, they discussed the prospects of their son and daughter's marriage proposal. They first started by expressing great concern about the harvesting of the rice on their farms.

They would send an invitation to the famous rice harvesters from the other villages to come to their aid Kpannah advised Tewa, since they were blessed with an abundance of rice on the farm that season.

"Um-hum!" nodded Tewah as she cautiously lifted her eyes and looked across the horizons at the vast acres of planted rice that waited to be harvested. "Oh! Yes, it's true, Kpannah. It's time that we ought to be getting prepared, since we are very fortunate that the God of the harvest has really blessed us this farming season. Even Chief *Gbekah Kondo* discussed the matter last night with the other elders in the village. They had planned to invite the mysterious and very dynamic reapers from Konyumodu village to come to our rescue."

"Ah! Tewa," said Kpannah, "someone told me about those wonderful men. I haven't seen them at work. What about you, Tewa, have you seen them at work?" she questioned her cautiously.

"Hum! Kpannah, it's one of the wonders of our time. An uncle who lived in that village many years ago during the harvest season invited me. They came to harvest the rice on his farm and I was very privileged to witness the spectacular scene," Tewa said. "I can't imagine how human beings could do such a difficult task with ease and with such pleasure and precision, as if joy was tinged with such haste and irritation. They were ten in number and mostly married men. Their wives and children also participated in the harvesting. They stood behind the men and offering them helping hands, giving them water to drink, kola nuts to make them agile, and cords made from loosed ropes they cut from trees, or peeled from stems of plants, to tie the sheaves of harvested rice when they requested them. They also sang sweet songs and the reapers continued their job with the tunes of joy of the songs."

"Eh! Tewa, our clan is renowned for such wonderful men who believe in charms and worship idols. They also believe that such idols help them greatly in the pursuit of their earthly ambitions," Kpannah said looking at Tewa and nodding her head.

Kpannah held her chin in the palm of her right hand and continued to listen in amazement as Tewa carried on telling her about the wonderful reapers.

"Kpannah," Tewah called her. "The reapers have certain laws which all of them have to abide. On the day of the harvest, no one is to stand ahead of them on the farm. They are accompanied to every acre of the farm by traditional praise singers, as well as drummers who play other native musical instruments. They all engaged in the activity with notable agility. They stood in a single line and faced the farm in one direction."

"Oh! Really?" Kpannah exclaimed, anxious to further such an interesting conversation.

"The image of the wonderful men already beamed from numerous successful expeditions they had had, throughout the clan. Oh! They must have been fortunate to be blessed by one of our highly renowned herbalists who died many years ago," Tewah said.

For even today, the procession of the wonderful reapers on farms in the Kissi land is the most interesting sight to see during the harvesting season. These were the most joyous days. The women and the others joined in singing the songs. Others narrated stories about ancient men and their exploits. In the midst of all that, *KaeNdeh*, a traditional musical instrument made from an old iron rod, that was knocked continuously, and accompanied with a heavy reggae and rap song, was the most appropriate for the occasion. The singer sang heavy rap music in stories and also divulged the folklore of the natives.

As he sang, feuds and vendettas were settled on the farms. Young men approached young women with sweet songs, and later got engaged and married. They then lay their own farms. At specific instances, the farmer who invited the reapers was fined. Such fines were paid in kola nuts, some kegs of the bamboo and palm wine, gin, and even dishes of cooked rice. It was great fun indeed. The reapers ate with their bare hands.

"Kpannah!"

"Eh! Is anything wrong, Tewa?"

"Oh! No! My dear, I called you to my farm today to discuss my son's proposal for your charming daughter," said Tewa. "Our family has met, and we have agreed for me to pursue all the appropriate arrangements for Tamba Kolloh to marry Kumba Mongor. We have already made sacrifices at the shrine of the Pela stream, and also at the oracle of the Ngebadu Hill, and prayed that God Almighty can bless us. We have already laid some kola nuts at the sacred place, where a huge rock comfortably sits on another rock on Ngebadu. We have also consulted with our psychics in Yilandu and even beyond. We have even met with Heiningbeh, the most famous of them all. They have all given us favorable responses, and we have done what they had wanted us to do. They have reiterated that it will be a very successful marriage, and that our forefathers are with us," she said contentedly.

Kpannah Mongor sat happily on an old log and looked at the vast acres of rice on the far horizon. A whirlwind blew dirt beside her and Tewa almost blowing off their head-ties. Small birds sang sweetly in the bushes around them. The women smelled the succulent rice that had passed the stage of virginity, and was ready to be harvested. Kpannah was well pleased and felt she was a very fortunate and happy woman, in whose possession was one of the most beautiful young women in Yilandu.

"You see, Tewa, I actually don't have much to say or any objection to such an amazing proposal," said Kpannah, continuing jokingly. "If Bandakillie Fugbu's great grandson wants to marry Nyuma Mongor's daughter, what should I say my dear? They are just following the path that our great grandparents left in the village and in Toli. It's actually very wise for our children to marry in our village, rather than sending our daughters to marry to distant places. Your son deserves success for the courage and persistence he has shown even in the face of discouragement. The entire clan is proud of his activities, especially his manly performance during the time of our bereavement. Tamba and Kumba should decide themselves and should devote all efforts to see that it works. I am very glad with your son, Tewa. You saw the way he boldly stood by our side and made our *Bolah* ashamed during the burial of my late husband."

They smiled and joked about the *Bolah*.

Kpannah continued, "The *Bolah* are all good-for-nothing people who only came to eat our food, joke and run away."

They giggled and made much fun of them.

"Tewa!"

"Eh!"

"Let me tell you," said Kpannah. "Tamba and Kumba are now so engaged to each other that no one could decide anything for them now. We should all pray that there shouldn't be any stumbling block in their marriage engagement. The old man has died a season ago today, and since then, your son has been there for us. He has really behaved towards us in a lambent humor. We love and also admire him."

As the conversation went on, Tewa Kolloh could really see victory and gave a tangible sigh of relief. They picked some corns, and they roasted them in the barn. Tewa then gave Kpannah some garden eggs, peppers and okras as gifts, to show great happiness in their discussion. She then put the vegetables and other provisions in a calabash, which Kpannah would return to her later when they came back to the village in the evening.

Hallie, Tamba Kolloh's little brother, was busy scaring birds on a high stand with a sling that his elder brother wove for him.

"Ha! Ah!" he yelled continuously.

The noisy palm and lovebirds wouldn't leave the rice plants, and so a few shots were fired with the sling in the same direction to scare the destructive birds. His mother and her friend could hear the shots above their heads.

"Hallie!" Tewa called. "Hallie-eh!"

"Eh! Ndeh." (Yes, Mom.)

"Look, you are firing your sling in our direction. You have to be very careful with your sling shots, okay," she admonished him.

"Where has your elder brother gone today?" she then demanded. "*Ndeh*! I saw brother Tamba going towards the village when the sun was about to stand erect in the sky," he said.

"Was he alone?"

"No! Ndeh, he was with Kumba Mongor. I think they went to look at his snares in the forest near Ngebadu," Hallie answered.

"Ha!" Tewa consented.

"Hah!" he again yelled continuously at the destructive birds on the high stand, his answer echoed into their ears like a roaring thunder.

The women stood speechless but were contented with everything, laughing and shaking their heads with admiration for their children. Never in the history of Yilandu had two people like Kumba Mongor and Tamba Kolloh come together to love and form such an everlasting union.

"Maybe, Tewa, they might be somewhere in the bushes around the village looking for fruits," Kpannah said.

"Oh! No, I believe Tamba might have taken her to see the new snares he laid few days ago in the forest near Ngebadu. He is very lucky with snares since he always makes good catches. He checks them very early in the morning to see if they caught any nocturnal animal," Tewa said with logical calmness.

"Tewa, your son is actually very lucky with snares. He once carried a bulky bush hog, which got trapped in one of his snares. He presented the entire carcass to me. I then called his wife, Kumba, to come to meet with him, and to thank him, but she was ashamed to come out-doors," Kpannah joked with a convivial laughter.

"Oh! My God! The husband carrying food for his wife and her family, but the wife runs away. How will she feed the family?" they said jokingly.

It was quite fun, and they continued to share such trifling jokes with pleasure and pride in what an industrious husband that Tamba Kolloh might be.

"Tewa, the sun is now extremely hot and has stood erect in the heavens, and since I left my children on their own scaring birds on the farm, I would love to return to check on them, and prepare some meal for them. Thank you for your kindness. I am greatly indebted to it," said Kpannah begging to leave.

"Oh, no, Kpannah! You are always welcome, my soon to be sister-in-law. I haven't started negotiating your daughter's bride- price yet," Tewa continued with a proud smile on her face.

"We shall talk more in the village where I will respond to your proposal," said Kpannah.

"Okay, Kpannah, and *e-dee-yoh (goodbye)*," said Tewa.

As Kpannah walked through the footpath that led to her farm, which was just half a mile away, she thought that it was indeed a joy that Tewa Kolloh had such a very loving, caring, handsome and bold son. She was also overjoyed about the vivacious courtesy shown her by her soon to be sister-in-law on her farm. The clouds changed in the sky and on the horizon; another gust of a whirlwind danced ahead of her. Such winds were more common in the savannah grassland; and where land and pastures, cows and cattle egrets, roam freely, in those areas in West Africa, and in other parts of the world. Though a natural phenomenon, it is interpreted differently by the Kissi.

"Um-Humm!" said Tewa out loud. "I am sure it's the spirit of my late husband that's always with me. Such funny winds bring messages from the dead to us, but we are not able to decipher their significance."

On one or two occasions, some cattle egrets sat ahead of her on the dusty footpath. She shook her head, took out a tiny snuffbox hidden from between her breasts and she inhaled from it three times. If she had sneezed several times, it would have indicated a bad omen. She bowed beside the edge of the footpath, and threw a few doses of snuff as a libation to the spirit of her late husband. Her eyes glittered with tears that ran down her fat cheeks. She smiled when she saw a toad hopping ahead of her on the dusty footpath.

"Maybe that should be Nyuma Mongor's ghost," she said looking at it cunningly and smiling a smile that didn't break the massiveness of her fat cheeks. She shook her head slightly, and entered the barn.

There she met her daughter, who had already started cooking the day's meal. Kumba Mongor had been with her future husband in the thick forest, where they luckily meet two snares that had captured a deer and an antelope. Tamba Kolloh had given her the choice to select one of the dead carcasses. She chose the antelope. He had told her that, if she were to get pregnant, she was going to bear a male child since she had chosen an antelope. It was the

Kissi peoples' belief. Her mother had found her roasting the carcass on the fire in the barn. She tried to burn the fur from its skin, and jerked as her mother entered the barn slowly, and unannounced, behind her.

"Eh! *Ndeh*, (Oh! Mother), you've really frightened me," she said.

"Kumba, I was very worried about where you had gone today, until Hallie, Tamba Kolloh's little brother, informed me and his mother that you were gone with him," she said.

"Oh! *Ndeh*, you went to *Ndeh* Tewa Kolloh's farm today?" she questioned.

"Yeah, I first of all passed to the other neighbor's farms where we have discussed the possibility of sending an invitation to the wonderful rice reapers from *Konyumodu village* to come to our rescue. If they don't, the rice will surely spoil on our farms this harvest season."

"That's very true *Ndeh*," Kumba said scrapping the fur off the dead animal carcass.

"Kumba!"

"Eh! *Ndeh*."

"Guess what?"

"What *Ndeh*?"

"See what your mother-in-law gave us today."

"Who is that, *Ndeh*?"

"You ought to know your mother-in-law by now, Madam Kumba

Mongor," her mother said.

"Tewa Kolloh, *Ndeh*?"

"Um-hum! She is exactly the very one that I am talking about. She is a very nice woman."

"*Ndeh*, her son, is very nice too," said Kumba Mongor.

"Of course, I can see the fat antelope in the calabash. We are going to eat it for over a week. We have to prepare it so that we can hang some meat in the makeshift heater above the fire in the barn.

"Okay *Ndeh*."

"Um-hum! My husband and my mother-in-law," Kumba said jokingly.

She sat down on a wooden stool and shook head gently, as she thought about it seriously, the other village lads who had chased her unsuccessfully passed through her mind. Her eyes were almost black with an impersonal hatred of the world that was now crushing her and her fiancée.

Most of the lads in Yilandu now eyed her with covetousness. She was the most beautiful and charming young woman among them and was also the most wanted woman among the youthful generation. She was honored everywhere she went for her charm and prettiness.

Korfeh, who was Tamba Kolloh's childhood friend, and with whom he had joined the Poro Society, now became one of his greatest enemies in the village. He had first shown great interest in Kumba, and had approached her to be his lover. He had, in fact, proposed to marry her but she had deceived him completely, and he was now very angry and stared at both Tamba and Kumba with hideous and malevolent intention every time he saw them.

Korfeh had also developed an animal instinct for extreme danger and had promised to fight Tamba Kolloh in the coffee and cacao plantation that surrounded the village, and also where the other village lads, and the old men went to play *Seeyon-yee-yoh* (spin-the-seeds game).

This game was played in the evenings, especially after the harvesting season in the villages in Kissi land. A couple of men who sat around a mound on which was placed a mat and the middle of the mound was dented to allow the seeds to spin considerably for seconds or a minute. The seed that knocks down one or more other seeds wins the game.

The seeds are made from hardwood, or sometimes made from the tusk of an elephant. They are round and with pointed heads so that spinning them with two or more fingers was easy. Winning was recognized when a seed went in the middle and knocked the other seeds to the ground. In certain instances, all the seeds fell, but the one that remained either spinning or static in the dent in the mound, was the winning seed. The exhilaration and the emotion that was evident when someone was proclaimed a winner were heard as far as in Yilandu.

Korfeh was very good at the game, in comparison; Tamba Kolloh was more of a hunter, a chief priest, and a daring young man in the village. Yet, sometimes, at leisure, Tamba Kolloh would play spin-the-seeds. Tamba had now grown into manhood and became wild—going on hunting expeditions alone, during the day and night, becoming one of the most renowned hunters in the Toli Clan. He was one of those very brave men who were called to hunt down even a tiger, a lion, a huge boa constrictor, or baboons when they became destructive, or when they were a threat to the clan.

The Kissi hunters were known far and wide for their daring exploits, often killing a lion or an elephant during such hunting expeditions. Hunting was perfectly done after the harvesting season. Yet, some very bold hunters went out every night to kill bush animals to bring food home for their families. They used headlamps that produced light using carbide, which they shook constantly to light.

Chief *Gbekah Kondo* had already dispatched emissaries to the chief of Konyumodu to arrange a date for the rice reapers to come to Yilandu. They had already consented and a date was set. Meetings had already been held in both villages. There were lots of volunteers who wanted their farms to be harvested by the "*Ngufeoyoh Rice Harvesters Club*," as they are called even today in Kissi land.

Two farms were to present a goat and a bag of cleaned rice as a present to the harvesters. It meant that Tamba Kolloh now represented two farms: his own and that of the late Nyuma Mongor. He then presented the items on their behalf. It was just a method to encourage the harvesters so that they could come whenever they were needed. They also extended that generosity to them due to their tradition.

The reaping of the rice harvesters was an important visit paid to their village, and so, they honored it with pride and dignity. *Yamba* the village crier had gone out to every hut and shouted to the inhabitants about the chief's decision. Early the next day, the people started to bring their contributions. Every household reared domestic animals. The village smelt of cow dung and the dirty pigs went helter-skelter, damaging the crops. They made the place very untidy and slippery, especially during the rainy season. Tamba Kolloh was the first to present what Chief Gbekah had requested, and so three farms were to be harvested on the same day: his farm, Chief Gbekah's farm, and the late Nyuma Mongor's farm.

At night in the village and in its outskirts, insects, birds, and other nocturnal animals continued to sing their noisy choruses. As usual, children rejoiced in the bright moonlight. They continued to play their games. Also, in the far swamps, frogs and toads sang drumming tunes. It was the drumming and the crowing of the roosters that woke the village early in the morning. When the clouds gave way to the moon, lovers too came out together to enjoy the cool breezes in the evening, chat about the countryside, and lay in each other's arms. Chokah again bumped into Tamba Kooloh.

"Eh! Chokah!"

"*Eseh*! *Ngore* (Big brother)," he greeted him.

"*A-cho-keNdeh*? (Are you alright?)" Tamba Kolloh questioned the little boy about his health.

"Eh! Kae-solar-Meleka-le (Thank God)," said Chokah. Thank God, he responded favorably about his health.

"Please go and call on Kumba for me, tell her to meet me in my hut," Tamba Kolloh commanded him.

"Eh! *Ngore*," you sent me the other day, but you didn't give me anything," Chokah grumbled noisily.

"Ok! *Falloh* (Sir)," said Tamba Kolloh. "Come for oranges and some fruits, but please make sure to perform my command successfully."

"*Ngore*! Just hang around and expect me to bring good news to you soon," he said, taking off on his heels immediately and disappearing between the mud huts. In less than a minute, he had emerged from Kumba Mongor's mother's hut.

Kpannah Mongor always met her little ones singing lullabies, and narrating stories in the moonlight. Their extended families and the next of kin were still coming in steady-streams to convey their deep sympathies over the death of the chief priest in the village. Such an important figure was mourned for years. Such relatives who came from those distant places entered into the village untidily from the outskirts, with bundles of clothes on their heads. They invariably loosed their hair, and left it unkempt, to look more like people in great frustration and sorrow for the death of a loved one.

A resurgence of grief swept the entire compound of the deceased. Even the children were told not to be very loud and noisy when playing with each other while such grief and condolences continued to pour from distant places.

Chokah had grown to become a competent emissary. He didn't jump on Kumba so rudely. Instead, he at first played with the children, and narrated funny stories to them, and when the singing started, and Kumba heard his voice, she then came out doors and he winked an eye at her. He twisted his head sideways, and looked at the direction of Tamba Kolloh's hut. Kumba Mongor then nodded and shook her head gently. When he had noticed that his duty was well performed, he left the site hastily and returned to inform Tamba Kolloh that his message had been successfully delivered.

"Did you see her, Chokah?"

"Urn-hum! *Ngore.*"

"She is on her way," he disclosed as he collected his

oranges and other fruits and then rejoined his colleagues to play the *Duduleng* (hide-and-seek-game) in the comers of the mud huts that were brightened by the rays of the moonlight.

When he left, Tamba Kolloh searched for his bottle lamp, and poured oil in it. He lit it, hid it behind the bed. He lay on his back and thought of the wonderful "*Ngufeoyoh Rice Harvesters.*" His mother had returned from the swamp where she went to look at the rice nursery she had planted. She saw a few patches that the destructive nocturnal animals and birds left. They also dropped lots of the succulent and some matured rice seeds on the ground. After she had inspected the destruction, she advised her son to make more snares around the swamp.

"Konk! Konk!" He heard a knock on the door.

"Who's that?" said Tamba Kolloh. No one answered at first. At the second knocking, he rose from the bed and opened the door slowly. A little black spotted cat he kept appeared cautiously, entered into the room briskly, and hid under the bed. It anxiously awaited any rat that would emerge from its hiding place.

At the door, Tamba and Kumba met. They smiled and hugged each other. Her sparkling and beautiful eyes shone in the darkness as if she were an angel—her beauty was beyond comparison to anyone in the village. Such visits occurred intermittently when she was not too occupied at home. Tamba was now very confident that his victory in finally winning her over was not a mere fluke but destined to happen confident of the shuttle diplomacy that gained grounds within the families in Yilandu. It was indeed an effective and truly genuine relationship. As she stood in his presence in modest consciousness of her own great powers, he felt that she was one of the loveliest, self-confident young women he had ever seen in the village. He held her hands and they sat abruptly on the bed.

The bouncing made the little black cat purr under the bed. It ran swiftly after a rat that had cunningly hidden from sight. Tamba and Kumba smiled at each other, and he closed the door with a long stick that he placed across it to hold it tightly.

"Humm! Chokah is very cunning and prudent in carrying out errands. He is very wise indeed," she said.

"Who? Chokah! That little cowboy! That's the reason that I love to send him on errands. He is actually highly intelligent in undertaking such tasks," he said.

"Eh! Tamba, our relationship has been discussed by every mouth in the village. Even most of your friends have now become our enemies. Take Korfeh, for instance. He has stopped talking to me these days," she said discouragingly.

"It's not only you, Kumba. He has attacked me on a number of occasions especially when we go to spin-the-seeds under the coffee and cacao trees on the outskirts of the village. He is always picking on me. Yet, I know all of our enemy's weak points. No one can boast of beating me. I am the strongest man in the village," he bragged.

"How do you know that, Tamba?"

"I used to beat all of them in the bush, when we joined the Poro Society some years ago. We used to wrestle a lot, and I was always the strongest. I can even beat two men at the same time. They all know that very well," he said boastfully.

"I know you might be the strongest man in the world, but I wouldn't appreciate you engaging in such brute acts in the village," she advised him.

"I won't, Kumba," he said reassuring her. "Realizing my position today as the chief priest, I will never engage in such brute acts again."

"Oh! Tamba, as a hunter, a chief priest, and with your kindness, you seemed to be a savior against all portending evil in the village. That has made the other villages like Palama, Kpangbening, Ye*Ndeh*, Maah, Kolobengu, Fodedu, etc., not only respect, but fear us today," she said.

He lay on his back and listened attentively to her enthusiastic impression of his exploits, looking continuously at the thatched ceiling made of sticks and dry grass, tied with twines collected from tree branches in the thick forest. The flames from the bottle lamp were dangling all over in the dark room. Kumba's feet were tired from hanging off the side of the bed. She told him to push aside, and slipped to lie comfortably beside him.

In the Kissi culture, woman lay behind their husbands on beds. Tamba then told her to move behind him. She agreed. He played with her breasts, which were already bulged, a sign of her passage into womanhood. Her voice too had dwindled significantly. It got so heavy that it seemed to have a bass echo.

"Tamba, I have to return home," Kumba said amiably. "I will not sleep here tonight since we are still getting distant mourners who come to pay condolences to us. My mother may like me to assist in doing home chores. Let's see now, so that I can be home sooner."

"Okay, it's very true," Tamba said sharply.

The oil lamp suddenly went off, and the rocking noises of the bed ensued. The dogs barked on the outskirts of the village. Cats purred. Distant owls hooted, and the thunderous noises of the countless insects echoed noisily all over their otherwise silent neighborhood. The children started catching the fowls and putting them inside the coops or *Sasah* (Kissi). These were special structures made of bamboo or palm fronds to house the fowls. The dogs and the dirty pigs always remained outdoors and acted as the night watchmen. The rocking of the bed stopped after a while. Tamba and Kumba lay on their backs tiredly.

"Tamba!" she called out quietly.

"Humm!" he pretended to be snoring.

"Look, the children are now catching the fowls. It's time to go to bed. May I go home now?" she asked politely.

"Okay, Kumba, but make sure to pass by in the morning with the items we previously talked about, so that we can carry them for the sacrifice at the shrine under the kola nut tree. I believe that by doing so, your father's soul may rest in peace," he cautioned her.

"Good night, Tamba."

"Bye, Kumba, and have sweet dreams," she said and boldly stepped outside neatly tying her head tie. He accompanied her, but stayed some distance behind. After she had passed two huts, she slipped into a neighbor's hut.

Sia Focko was her childhood friend. She met her and they discussed Tamba Kolloh's intention for her. She also explained to Sia how she had become a target by the rude lads in the village.

"Kumba," said Sia Focko. "You don't have to listen to those stupid fools. You don't have to live the way others want you to live. They only want to discourage or frighten you. Just take my situation, for instance. They said lots of evil things concerning my husband, Sahr, and me. But today, we have our own hut, lay our own farm, and have our own children. You should know that we are living in a very tight community. Some see more evil in you than good. Go home. Let's discuss it tomorrow since it's getting too late," she advised her.

"Okay, Sia Focko, I will see you tomorrow."

"Bye, Kumba Mongor."

That night, Kumba couldn't sleep very well. She thought about her adventures in life for the first time. Why should she have enemies so quickly in her life? It would have been better for her to remain a virgin than to engage in such man-business, an escapade that had ended with such disastrous consequences. Before she slept that night, she poured some handfuls of cleaned rice in a small calabash and poured some water on the rice. She was to pour the soaked rice in a mortar and pound it with a pestle the next day, and get it ready for the sacred sacrifice. That night, she felt an urge to stand on her legs. She woke her mother up, and told her the same.

"Do you want to stand on your legs Kumba?" her mother questioned her drowsily.

"Eh! *Ndeh.*"

Kpannah opened the door, and Kumba stood on her

legs. The stars and moon that stitched up in the sky illuminated the corners of the village so brightly that someone could pick up a pin on the ground. The dogs continued to bark on the outskirts of the village as a long moment of hushed silence blanketed the entire clan.

"Kumba, those dogs don't bark for nothing. They see mysterious images and other inanimate objects that human beings can't see with their eyes," her mother disclosed matter-of-factly, frightening her daughter.

They hurriedly entered into the hut and closed the door behind them. Before they slept, they heard the distant shots from a hunter's gun fired in the forest. They slept, tired from working all day long on the farm. Kumba had never explained to her about the rude behavior that the village lads were displaying towards her. She had not wanted her mother to believe that she was weak, and had no self-control or respect. Therefore, she kept things to herself—always at pains to project a good image.

Kumba woke early the next day, put the soaked rice in a mortar and pounded it with a pestle until it turned into flour, which had sacred and useful purposes in making sacrifices at the shrines and oracles in the village. She then peeled some fresh kola nuts and placed some handfuls of the flour she had made into small morsels in the form of round balls in a small calabash, and hurried to Tamba Kolloh's hut.

He had just woken up but still felt tired to rise. He lay like a sack of rice on the bed. A dim and hazy light greeted his slowly opening eyes when he heard a knock on the door. Tamba knew that it was Kumba, and that they were to be ready to fulfill the ceremony under the sacred kola nut tree. After putting on his sacred country-cloth shirt and short country-cloth trousers, he collected a few sacred bottles filled with exotic herbs, some ancient idols, kola nuts, a small bottle of cane juice, a red hen, a small knife, a small harp and lots of other sacred items needed for such sacrifices. They hurriedly left the village and entered into the forest by using the back entrance of Tamba Kolloh's hut.

A green snake crossed swiftly on the footpath ahead of them and it disappeared into the shrub.

"Oh! Tamba—that's Dad's ghost accompanying us," she whispered when she saw it. Her face beamed with a subtle smile.

"Of course," said Tamba. "You see, Kumba, there is life after death. I have dreamt of my late father Sakillah Kolloh. He comes in my dreams and advises me to fulfill one or two sacrifices for the welfare of the family. Whenever I perform them, we are enriched with pleasant fortunes. I did the same before we planted rice on our farm. Today, the acres of rice are so vast on the farm that we have invited reapers from Konyumodu to come to our aid."

"Eh! Tamba, I just knew that you were a posthumous child. How did you know that the ghost that appeared in your dreams was your father's?" she asked him appearing dismayed.

"Well, Kumba, any sensible person knows their father when they see a picture of him. I once discussed the matter with my mother and I described him to her. She told me that it was definitely my father. He was black, slim, and very handsome indeed. He had sleepy-eyes, and it's exactly the same person that I see every day."

"Hum!" said Kumba. "It's true Tamba. You have your father's sleepy eyes." Tears gushed from her eyes.

"It's fate, Kumba. We all have to die someday."

"You know what Tamba?"

"What?"

"Hum! We have mothers but no fathers," she said sadly.

"Well, it's how the world goes. God has called them, and I know that they are resting in *Aljenneh* (Heaven).

There were several cults in the clan. Each was represented by an idol. The idols were placed at shrines and at oracles, and libation was poured on them so that they could fulfill special dispensations in their lives. Tamba Kolloh's shrine was under the famous kola nut tree. It was there that he was to be directed by the gods to perform rituals according to their directives and with the supernatural powers that they gave him. It was also there that he was to display the sacred art to reflect the values of the Kissi society with beauty and splendor. In the ancient times, such rituals were performed with mysticism.

Under the giant kola nut tree, Tamba and Kumba had already met several mystic objects and other exotic charms magnificently displayed by some unknown ghosts or UFOs. They wondered who had brought the sacred items and neatly placed them there. Tamba took a deep, tremulous breath and relaxed slightly. But Kumba Mongor's eyes were horror-stricken and she opened her mouth to scream. A very huge boa constrictor had wrapped itself high up in the kola nut tree. Kumba, profusely sweating, was already drenched with perspiration. She and Tamba stood speechless. Yet, what they were about to experience was indeed never easy to elucidate.

Two golden rings fell from the tree and, amidst everything a mysterious voice was heard while Tamba Kolloh played a mysterious tune on the harp. He had been taught the song in his dream.

The voice said, "To you the young, it's still Nyuma Mongor speaking to you on this day. Each of you should take the golden ring and put the ring on the middle finger of your left hand. The *Domah* (the most powerful idol) or charm will assist you to elucidate important mysteries that have been lost in the midst of time. Your activities in Yilandu and the Toli Clan will ever be remembered, and shall be told in stories. The griots shall sing these mysteries in the golden age of advanced civilizations. Your mystic charms will be prodigious. You shall be loved by the denizens of other planets. They shall also help you divulge ancient mysteries and people shall come in steady streams from all over the world to visit your shrine, and seek your help."

They stood and listened intently but took tremulous breaths. A liquid-like substance was poured on their heads from high above the tree, and the mysterious voice continued: "Rub every inch of your body with this mysterious liquid. It's a charm to make you invincible to all awful human machinations. Continue with your ritual, and return to the village triumphantly," the mysterious voice concluded.

They thanked the ghost as it disappeared mysteriously.

Tamba then bent on his knees and Kumba sat on a dry log beside him. The rays of the rising sun penetrated the uncountable cacao and coffee leaves. It shone directly on Tamba Kolloh's forehead. He tilted his head sideways just to discourage the rays from shinning directly in his face. He then began to mumble a long and an involved incantation as he played the harp:

"Oh! God of the rivers, God of the mountains, and God of our oracles and shrines! God of our forefathers! We have come to feed you today bearing gifts with open hearts and with every polite convention befitting our Kissi culture so that you can open our chances for every success during the harvest. We pray for the welfare of our kinsmen in Yilandu and in the Toli Clan. Keep us free from sicknesses, calamities and all other evils—*Ameee-nah*!" the both of them answered.

They then put the kola nuts and the morsels of the white flour in a small calabash and placed all the items at a vantage location under the giant kola nut tree. Tamba also decorated them with idols, bottles and other exotic herbs and ointments. They stood, bowed their heads, closed their eyes, and recited a goodbye incantation to the inanimate objects, which had now become living idols by the power of their mystic incantations. They turned around and left the site.

Neither of them turned back until they were on the outskirts of the village. The spot under the kola nut tree then became Tamba Kolloh's mysterious shrine from that day.

They could now feel their faces beaming proudly. The

clan was filled with very brave men and women. Some of them had gone early to their graves as easy prey to superstitious beliefs. As they reached the outskirts of the village, the dogs barked, and the fowls crowed, which signified the entering into the village by a prodigious herbalist and chief priest.

Tamba and Kumba were to become the architects that could wipe the tears of the idols in the village, and were also going to propound the truth of a mysterious spiritual evolution in the Toli, and beyond. They were going to be respected as deities and heroes and their superb works would be ever remembered in the spiritual annals of the Kissi land.

They now became fond of each other. Early one morning, Tamba Kolloh discovered ten cowry shells that he was to display with his fingers on a small mat. These shells were to make him a renowned psychic in the clan, in his day.

His fame soon spread like a wild fire that ravaged a dried harmattan bush. He was asked to advise the elders about the culprits that engaged in cannibalism, witchcraft or sorcery as the death of their chief priest Nyuma Mongor. The same culprits made ghastly evils to germinate wildly in all villages in Toli and beyond. Tamba Kolloh was to become the most successful psychic and herbalist in his day in Yilandu, and he was feared by others who claimed to have had the same supernatural powers in distant lands.

CHAPTER FOUR

The harvest was near. The reapers had already arrived in Yilandu. Chief *Gbekah Kondo* called a meeting of all the elders and the various households in the village. They had discussed the lodging arrangements for their very famous guests and visitors, and also made the schedule of how the harvesting was to take place. They now met to negotiate a peaceful settlement. Since they considered seniority in their culture, the chief's farm was to be harvested first.

Drummers and praise singers had already been called and had started to entertain the guests and visitors. Villagers joined in the festivities too. Drummers and singers were given gifts in kind. Kola nuts were shared to demonstrate to their visitors how happy and very proud they all were. Young and the old danced to the traditional music. Native singers in their songs taught them about love, bravery, ancient heroes in the clan and their wonderful deeds and endurance. The splendors of the beauties of old were eulogized. Lead singers yelled the names of some important figures in their clan, and the others eulogized such names in stories untold before.

The crowd echoed in thundering applause. It was in the midst of such dances that *Yamba* the greatest griot in Yilandu yelled, and there was silence. He told them that the chief was on his legs.

"My compliments, venerable elders, our most gifted reapers, ladies and gentlemen," began Chief *Gbekah Kondo.* "It's time that I officially inform all of you about the arrival of our dynamic guests from Konyumodu to Yilandu."

The crowd echoed in thundering applause again. *Yamba* cooled them down with another funny song.

The chief continued, "They are here for a very short time since they are requested in other villages of our clan. They will commence their work tomorrow. You can as well see the cozy arrangements that have been made in the village just to welcome them, and to show them that we highly recognize their presence here today."

Yamba yelled a few praises for the mighty Chief *Gbekah Kondo*. He called him the elephant and the lion of Toli.

The chief continued amid thundering applause, "Since the rice is so ripe on our farms and the heavy seeds have started falling from their weak steams, the elders have agreed that my farm and Tamba Kolloh's farm will be harvested as scheduled tomorrow."

The crowd echoed again, which permitted the chief to gather the huge arms of his country cloth gown, and put them around his shoulder. He waved for the traditional drummers and singers to officially commence their performances. Kola nuts were again shared in small calabashes, and *Yamba* continued with his praises.

The head of the wonderful reapers was a frail old man called Sokoh. He was a respected old man who sat in the chief's shed. He was presented with some kegs of the best palm and bamboo wine, as well as some bottles of *Tamba Nanjahn gin (cane juice)*. He nodded to every word that the chief and his kinsmen said of the wonderful deeds of his outstanding band of reapers. He had known *Yamba* for quite a very long time and knew that he was a very witty storyteller, whose teachings in funny songs were loved by everyone in the entire clan. People came in large crowds to any farm that *Yamba* went just to be in his company.

"Oh! Sokoh, there are men among men," *Yamba* yelled praises for him.

"Hum! This great lion of Konyumodu—by this time tomorrow, his men will be hammering the huge acres of rice on the farms…for even Piomdo (god of prosperity and harvest) shall sit on his thrown tomorrow and smile at the greatest deeds of these very wonderful reapers. Their praises already beam from their countless exploits on ancient farms throughout the clan. They also get modest courage from their kinsmen," said *Yamba,* concluding the eulogy.

The onlookers fought their way amid the large crowd by pushing others just to see Sokoh. He and his men had been given the loftiest praises by their most trusted and very versatile griot. Those were the rewards and recognition that *Yamba* poured on anyone he praised.

Tamba Kolloh's fame had grown very wild within days, later that day; a little girl was rushed into his hut. The parents lay her unconscious body on a mat. She vomited blood and her eyes were closed tightly and she cried with spasms of pain allover her body.

"Oh! Tamba Kolloh," Sindoh, the girl's mother, cried hysterically. "Tamba Kolloh, my daughter Tuwoh is dying. Oh! God help me. Do something!"

"What's wrong with her, *Ndeh*? (Mother)," he questioned respectfully.

"Oh! Tamba Kolloh, she was scaring birds on the farm and she fell down and started vomiting white flush from her mouth and nostrils," said Sindoh.

Tamba Kolloh immediately sat on his mat and took his cowry shells. He threw them on the mat and looked cunningly at the pattern that was made by the cowry shells. He then touched each shell with a finger and displayed them to make more patterns on the mat. He shook his head proudly as the most gifted psychic of his time. He smiled since the shells illustrated signs whose meanings he could well divulge.

"Ah! Ha! *Ndeh* Sindoh, your daughter was knocked heavily on the head by a very powerful and evil voodoo man. He had envied the little girl and really wanted to take her life. The idol used in such a very fatal attack is called *Sambeiyoh* (a deadly god that kills instantly).

"Oh! Tamba, my son, please save my poor daughter's life. I beg you my son. I beg you," she repeated over and with faint yells in between. Her eyes brimmed with clouds of tears, which she wiped with her head tie.

Her cries touched his kind heart. He rose from the mat and opened an earthen pot. Taking out some black liquid, he poured on the little girl's face, while reciting a mysterious incantation. A white powder was also rubbed all over the girl's body, while he called on the gods of his ancestors; and for the guidance of God Almighty, and asked them humbly to rescue the poor girl from the shackles of death.

After a few minutes, he was to exorcise the evil spirit in her. With a twinkle, the girl opened her eyes but couldn't move because she felt too haggard and very sleepy but she screamed for her mother to hold her hand. Tamba Kolloh told Sindoh not to touch her daughter until the evil spirit had left her completely. He sent a cat to the bushes on the outskirts of the village and it returned with several exotic herbs in its mouth, which he smashed in a calabash and poured. Some ointment was added to the herb pulp. The little girl drank his liquid as he recited another mysterious incantation in time.

As he rubbed the leaves all over her body, she woke immediately and sat by her own strength on the mat. She looked around her dizzily and baffled, unable to comprehend what had really happened to her. It was like a dream. Her mother sat beside her with her mouth wide open. She nodded her gray head in a very pleasing manner, though she was still frightened.

The onlookers who sat in the hut and those who looked from the windows of the hut were greatly surprised. Kemah clearly remarked that Yilandu was from generation to generation blessed with men and women gifted with such supernatural powers send by the gods to cure illnesses. She sat in the hut and looked at the wonders that had occurred in her presence.

The Kissi considered such very wonderful men and women deities, sent to them by their forefathers to perform such miracles among them. From that day, their affection for Tamba grew more and more, and was deeply genuine, tinged with great admiration.

Chief *Gbekah Kondo* was then informed about the episode. He was accompanied to Tamba Kolloh's hut by some of the elders in the village. They hung their heads as Sindoh explained to them what had taken place. The little girl and her mother had gone home when the girl was able to stand on her legs. From that very day, Tamba Kolloh started to realize that all Nyuma Mongor's ghost had told him came to pass like a revelation.

His hut now became a melting pot for all supernatural beliefs and power in the Yilandu. Even those who came with their problems from distant clans found rightful solutions in Tamba Kolloh's hut or shrine under the kola nut tree. Those who searched for fortunes and more came, and he gave them sacred idols in the forms of amulets, rings and other tokens. They returned to their distant villages, and mysteriously abundance came.

The women who were barren and wanted to bear children came too. He took them to a special shrine in the swamp near the Pela or Boon stream, and there he laid some kola nuts and scared herbs to *Koeh* (god of fertility). The women were washed and when they returned home, they reported bearing children. Also, women who never had husbands called out to this wonderful psychic, and their prayers were answered.

Hunters who went to hunt in the deep forest at night came to him for special charms that could make them invincible. The charms also protected them against attacks from ferocious and ruthless beasts like the tigers, lions, and elephants, and boar constrictors. Tamba Kolloh's supernatural powers couldn't be explained because they were beyond human comprehension.

Tamba's hut was now an impenetrable fortress for evil and supreme supernatural beings, as well as those of good fortunes. They appeared to him and they performed rituals. Even the most powerful of the witches and wizards, and other evil juju men and woman in the village, came to his hut surreptitiously and begged him not to disclose them to their kinsmen. Some brought kola nuts and other provisions harvested on their farms. With his charms, he cured them in Almighty God's name.

Tamba's hut was the most fearful den in the entire clan. He was indeed the most powerful chief priest ever to live among them. Those who tried to invade his fortress through sorcery died immediately in the attempt unless he pardoned them. That was why the young men and women who had attempted to penetrate his impregnable fortress went early to their graves.

Invincible boas, lions, and other deadly and poisonous denizens now manned the fortress, always ready to attack any intruder at Tamba's command. Tamba also had a cat at his command, which the Kissi considered to be very sacred.

Kumba Mongor helped Tamba Kolloh sometimes. She also had the same powers, but in Kissi culture, the man was always the head of such a fortress. Kumba and Tamba had agreed to be married immediately after the harvest season. They remained lovers, and they never disclosed of how they became very famous to any living being. It was the law, and they adhered to it strictly. The disclosure of such a secret meant instant death for both of them.

The sun had fallen over the horizon and dusk was fast approaching. The drummers played and the reapers had long gone to bed. One could hear the sound of the drums, like the *Tambalan* and *Samgbalan*, with the shakers and *Yamba*'s voice that sang solo, as the festivities continued in the village.

In the late night, Tamba Kolloh heard a knock on his door. There was great silence. The black cat could tell exactly who was on the other side of the door; it purred and yearned, trying to make faint barks like a dog. The village psychics were accustomed to visitors coming to them at any time in the evening hours and welcomed them.

"Who's that?"

"It's me, Tamba."

"Oh! *Ndeh* (Oh! mother), Sindoh?"

"Eh!"

"Oh! My son, I came purposely to thank you for saving my poor daughter's life," she said sitting on the mat and holding her feet passionately together. Her eyes were brimming with tears.

"*Ameee-nah*!" Tamba said thanking her.

"Thank you, my son. I am a poor woman, and I don't have anything to repay you, but God Almighty shall bless and guide you to live long in our village," she said, her soft, gentle voice shaken with sobs.

"*Ameee-nah*!" Tamba said again.

"We shall ever continue to praise you for your bravery and your tactical genius in comprehending so quickly our medicine in the form of roots, leaves and barks of medicinal trees and shrubs. Tamba, your quiet and retiring nature and your abhorrence of any kind of failure in executing your greatest deeds in our clan will ever remain etched in our memories. May the God of some of our most prominent forefathers like Bandakillie Fugbu, Barkeley, Pusuh, Hoorloh, guide you today."

"*Ameee-nah*!" Tamba answered.

"You are as all those who performed such wonderful deeds in our clan and who divulged such mysteries and practiced them long ago, which have remained spiritually," Sindoh continued. "May our forefathers pour more spiritual powers on your shoulders and also bless your sacred idols, that you should continue to reign and to also attack and to destroy all evils not only in our village, but in the entire Toli Clan."

"*Ameee-nah*!" Tamba Kolloh said once more.

He looked at his cowry shells.

"Ndeh Sindoh, your daughter Tuwoh was knocked on the head by an old man, dark in complexion and who nurses the idol of dragon we call, *Sambeiyoh*," he said turning the shells over and over again and noticed other strange signs.

"What, Tamba! You said very dark in complexion?" she repeated. "Is he slim too?" she continued to question him earnestly.

"Yes, *Ndeh* Sindoh, and the gods are telling."

Tamba was asked to advise the elders about the culprits that engaged in cannibalism, witchcraft or sorcery, after the death of their chief priest, Nyuma Mongor, those who made the same evils disseminate wildly in all villages in Toli. Yet, Tamba Kolloh was to become the most successful psychic during his day in Yilandu and he was also feared, too.

"Oh! No! It's Dundoh. The old man is presently on my farm. He had been helping me to harvest my farm these days. He must be the very one, since he jokes with her always. She is fond of him, too. I shall meet him on the farm tomorrow," she asserted in great annoyance. "Um-Humm!"

"Tamba!"

"Eh! *Ndeh*."

"I really have to tell you something confidentially."

"Go ahead *Ndeh*."

The village was now almost deserted. There was still some sound from *Yamba*'s small shaker, as the elders continued to sit and share fun with him in Chief *Gbekah Kondo*'s shed. There were kegs of palm wine.

Bending, she lowered her voice and said secretly, "You see, Tamba, our village is filled with charms most of us inherited from our grandparents, who left such idols with us in the family. Most of us inherited them when we were young, innocent children. We couldn't distinguish between good and bad. I would therefore like for you to be my protective armor or my umbrella in the village. We fear you because you are now our father. You are the most powerful, most invincible and the most spiritually gifted herbalist in our clan today. It's because of this that all of us fear you greatly," she said closing her mouth respectfully.

"*Ndeh* Sindoh, I've understood all that you have said," answered Tamba. "It's okay with me, *Ndeh* Sindoh. My law is that no one hurts innocent children, who are most vulnerable to such evil acts in the clan. I am planning to launch a *witch-hunt* in the village pretty soon, to stop ruthless men and women from hurting little children. They have become a threat since the death of Nyuma Mongor in the village. Since most of you have confided in me, and will no longer engage in such evil acts, never to break the promises you have all made to me, I won't have any problem stopping it," he stressed firmly.

"Okay, Tamba," said Sindoh. "It's getting dark and I have to hurry home to catch few hours of rest before the hectic work on the farm tomorrow."

"Goodbye, *Ndeh* Sindoh."

"Bye, Tamba."

Kumba Mongor had stood at the window in the late night. She heard every word of the conversation that went on between Tamba Kolloh and the old woman in the hut by looking at them through a chink in the mud wall. As they said their good-byes, Kumba withdrew to a considerable distance where she waited for Sindoh to depart. She was actually a very softhearted person, but jealousy has no boundaries. The quarrelsome attitude she developed sometimes was due to her inexperience in life's pursuits. The delay the old woman in Tamba's hut made her angry.

As another point of Kumba's jealousy, Tuwoh, *Ndeh* Sindoh's daughter, was also very beautiful and younger than Kumba Mongor. Kumba suspected that the old woman was trying to convince Tamba Kolloh to turn his attention to her daughter instead of her, since he had saved her life, or to get a second wife. In the Kissi culture, men sometimes became engaged even to babies or very young girls, who they helped to raise, and later became their suitors and married them in their teenage years.

Kumba stood and took an awful look through the chink in the mud wall, and soon realized that she was a stupid woman. She then gave an unconcerned gesture and waited until they had finished their conversation.

Immediately after the old lady left, Kumba briskly entered into the hut without any courtesy. She sat on the bed and gave a very sultry smile, which smelt of jealousy.

"*Eseh*! (How are you?) Kumba," Tamba Kolloh greeted her.

"What did she come to do at this hour of the night?" she questioned him with very stern eyes.

"Ah! Kumba, a jealous woman really has no common sense. Both of us have started an adventure fraught with disastrous consequences if we fail. You know that a dragon controlled by an old man in the village struck her daughter, and we cured her. She then came to thank us for what we did for her daughter, and to negotiate an understandable settlement with the idols in her possession," he said.

"Tamba, to negotiate what?" she questioned him very rudely with a disdainful pout on her face.

"Look! Kumba, she is actually one of those who we can't take for granted. Yet she has come out openly to beg that we be her protectors in the village."

"Oh! Tamba," she said. "So you never knew that she was one of those witches in the village? It would have been better for her daughter to die. It's the same she might have done to others' children over the years in Yilandu. What goes around comes around," she added angrily.

"Of course Kumba, yet, we don't have to be too petulant over issues that might or might not have taken place. We don't have any proof. Now is our time, and it's the time that we set a good example in the village since I have decided to go on a *witch-hunt* soon," said Tamba. At the same time, he bowed in a plea.

They soon jumped into other jokes, and Kumba voiced what she had expected openly. "Tamba, I don't really care if you love Tuwoh or if you make her your second wife."

Kumba laid her back on the hard bed and laughed derisively at the joke she had made, "Kumba, how did you come up with that?"

"It's your business Tamba. I don't actually care about it," she said.

He then lay beside her and touched her breasts. They were lost in each other's arms. Dark clouds had long hid the stars, and the village was now very quiet. The moon fought to send its brilliance to the earth. Even the drummers and the shakers players that entertained the villagers in the evenings had quieted, and gone to their early sleep since they had a hectic day ahead of them and they needed to store energy for their performance. He continued to touch Kumba but she rejected his touches with repugnance. She continued to be vexed at such antics.

"Um-hum! Never trust another woman with your boyfriend," she joked.

Yet Tamba wasn't angry. Kumba was just showing how immature she was, he thought. He continued to play with her breasts until she smiled pleasantly. He told her that they should be delighted with the pride and fame they had achieved over a short period because of the assistance they continued to give to their kinsmen, who were so excited with their accomplishments, and always sending their compliments to them.

Immediately, when they were again well adjusted in bed,

she complained to him.

"Eh! Tamba," said Kumba. "I have not seen a moon. It has already passed and I have missed it. I am feeling funny too."

He lay for a while on his back, looked up to the ceiling, and wondered. It was the first time that a woman ever had told him about "missing a moon."

"Kumba! What do you mean by saying that you missed a moon?" he said, and smiling at the same time.

She again smiled and studied the hazy light produced by the oil lamp on the mud wall, and ceiling of the thatched roof.

"Any man that doesn't understand such a figurative expression is not yet matured," said Kumba. "Tamba, you said that I was not quite matured because of my jealousy, but I am not. I didn't mean that I did not see the actual moon in the sky, but that I didn't see my period last month."

"Oh! Ho! Look! Kumba, I was really lost with what you were saying. I have just understood everything now. I am also very contented to hear such good news," Tamba said broadening his smile. "I will be very happy to be a very proud father and will be considered venerable among my kinsmen in Yilandu and in Toli. I will now own my own compound and have children. Thank you sincerely, Kumba," she added happily.

"Now you understood everything," she said relieved. "But look, Tamba, I am tired and want to go home now."

"Okay, the reapers will be on my mother's farm tomorrow. Don't forget to come over to give a helping hand," he said.

"I know about that already, and I have told my mother about it too. She has consented to it. Please expect me in the morning," she said assuring him.

She was still too tired to get off the bed. The oil lamp went off. And they slept until in the early hours of the morning, when she woke, dressed, and marched with heavy steps to her mother's hut. She was now a very bold woman and though, very proud, and commenced to openly show her love for Tamba Kolloh, and to stick to it.

Yamba Yilandu was the only griot in the clan that never slept. The barking of the village dogs and the crowing of the fowls greeted the echo of his baritone voice in the eerie morning hours. The noisy choruses of the frogs and toads in the distant swamp signified the break of day. *Yamba* then cleared his throat, and declared loudly:

"To all the sons and daughters of Yilandu, it's me, *Yamba*, informing you that our dynamic and tireless reapers from Konyumodu will commence their reaping on Chief Gbakeh Kondo's farm today. They will also work on Tamba Kolloh's farm today. The chief is asking all versatile and strong men and women to be on those farms to give a helping hand to them. I will be there too. Please come over with your harvesting knives. There will also be singers and drummers on both farms. We are all to assemble on Chief *Gbekah Kondo*'s farm. Please come all, to make it a great and a very historic day in Yilandu. Thank you."

Yamba also a village crier, stopped in every compound and every corner of the village repeating the speech over and over. The dogs that guarded him accompanied him barking noisily. The cows mooed intermittently as they scattered their dung all over in the village.

The villagers had woken and opened the doors of their mud huts. Yet, their famous griot continued his announcement unabated even though the village was now brisk with human activities. Chief *Gbekah Kondo's* many wives had woken earlier, and Sofedu, the head wife, had arranged for the cooking of a sumptuous meal in the chief's compound.

Some wives had placed some large pots on three huge rocks. Other wives blew the fire under the pots with their breath just to blaze it as the dry wood ignited. When it was hard to start the fire, they fanned the dry wood with large woven palm, which they used to winnow rice in, until the fire blazed under the pots.

Two goats had been slaughtered, and several fowls were killed. They cooked the most delicious sauce, which was most common on such important days, cassava and potato leaves sauce. Tewah Kolloh joined with Chief *Gbekah Kondo*'s wives, and they all cooked together. Kpannah Mongor was now her best friend and soon to be her sister-in-law. Kpannah joined them, too. The women exchanged exuberant greetings, and worked in unity.

Chief *Gbekah Kondo*'s farm, the largest in the village, was already congested early that morning with reapers, singers and helpers. He was their most powerful and famous chief, and he was most feared in the entire Clan. Others came to the farm on that day, only to see Tamba Kolloh, whose fame had already gone far and wide because of his mystic powers.

The reapers had already been divided into two groups, and were also assisted by their kinsmen from the other villages. Many bottles of their locally produced gin, *tamba Nanjahn (Cane Juice),* were shared among the reapers. There were also enough kegs of palm and bamboo wine as well. The liquor however made some of the farmers tipsy and some intoxicated, but it also made them very happy, and they performed their tasks with agility.

Early that morning on the chief's farm, the chief and the other elders held a small ceremony. Kendema, one of the venerable elders, well versed in reciting special incantations during ceremonies, held a small bottle of the locally produced gin, and they prayed on it.

He then poured it at a secret location on the farm as a libation to *Piomdo* (god of prosperity) to thank him for such abundance in their food production. Kendema then squatted on the ground and recited a long incantation that ended in a long, "Ameee-nah!"

During this ceremony, they also praised God and the names of the forefathers who had died long ago and had played important roles in their lives in the clan, behind this, the sound of the talking-drums, and *Yamba*'s voice echoing. The singers also joined in and they raised their soprano and tenor voices. They eulogized the names of their brave men and women who had died long ago in the clan.

The Ngufueyoh Reapers Club organized the long lines of reapers on both farms. They stood in front of the other helpers and reapers. No one stood in front of the wonderful reapers. They reaped as fast as a robot machine and wore specially made hats decorated with idols in the form of amulets.

No human being could comprehend how they actually did their job. They were the robot machines in the Kissi land. Palm and bamboo wine flowed in abundance. The reapers had brought down enough kegs from their bamboo and palm trees, they reaped so fast, and at the same time they constantly rocked their heads to the rhythm of the songs and the drums played on the farm, never stopping.

Later, Tewah Kolloh's farm was also crowded. The visitors had been ravenously eager to see her wonderful son. Tamba's fame had spread like the rays of the sunlight all over the Kissi land. He had appeared earlier on the farm and sprinkled an exotic liquid in a clay pot with a tail of an unknown animal and had also gone to his shrine to feed the idols there. The sacred sacrifices were made to fight against anyone who could have thought of harming the reapers, helpers and even the singers. This was common among the Kissi; a witch sending a snake to bite someone on the farm or to cause the havoc, just to delay the harvesting, could do such harm.

The reapers had made two long harvesting arcs, and they planned to encircle the farms before the sun rose above the heads. The drums continued to echo, and the very tuneful voices and songs poured over the workers. On Tewah Kolloh's farm *Yamba* yelled and told everyone gathered to note that they were on the farm of a young, charming and dynamic lady whose son was now the most illustrious and energetic deity, and an architect of the spiritual revolution in the clan.

He narrated ancient stories of the village and clan, and

how Tamba Kolloh's grandfather, Bandakillie Fugbu, used to tie baboons and hunt boa constrictors alone on Ngebadu. He told them that the gods of old had returned to physical human form as they were seeing in his grandson, Tamba Kolloh, who had clearly proved the truth of reincarnation, which was also acknowledged among the Kissi.

At any time *Yamba* yelled, he got a huge applause from the large crowd on both farms that lay adjacent each other. The griot was presented with gifts, like kola nuts, gin, and food. He looked upon Tamba Kolloh with great admiration, and the young and old loved him for his great knowledge in their culture and his spiritual and historical ostentation.

As *Yamba* continued to pour praises on Tamba, the children surrounded their greatest griot, also loving him for the witty stories he told. The drummers played nonstop music. The elders and others danced to the music, and some reapers who came to help, joined in singing the sweet songs. Jokes and stories accompanied the songs of old.

The laborers sweated profusely. The women took the sheaves or rice and tied them in small bundles with ropes peeled from loosed cords in the bushes and branches of trees on the farm. The sheaves of rice were then put into ties, and transported to the village by children on their heads and by the women in baskets.

As the sun was about to rise to its highest point in the sky, the job now become hectic, and *Yamba* became the main focus on the farm. He was the most prolific storyteller of their time. On Tewa Kolloh's farm, he loudly tried to share one of his funny stories with the reapers, elders, and helpers. He then narrated one of his funniest stories. The people listened to him attentively and he commenced:

"Once upon a time, Lappia was one of the most gifted hunters in Yilandu, and even in the entire clan. He took a very charming and a beautiful young woman as a concubine. She was called Lusuh. Her beauty also made her a target, wildly eyed by the young men in the village in those days. She was very fond of him, too, because of her innocent age.

"Lappia was a very jealous man. He never stayed long or overnight chasing animals during his hunting expeditions in the forest. He often returned home unannounced, thinking that Lusuh was going to be fooled by the young men, who had also shown great love for her in the village. It was actually a situation that always caused an occasional flash of disharmony between Lappia and the village lads, because of his very pretty and vivacious wife. He then decided to marry her. He called her relatives together, and he paid an enormous bride price for her. He even gave her relatives cows, goats, tins of oil, and sacks of cleaned rice, gold, and lots of other expensive items. She now officially became his wife.

"At any time he decided to go on a hunting expedition to a far distance, he always returned home abruptly, to see if Lusuh was engaged in any promiscuous behavior. He would then lie to her that he had caught a trifling cold in the eerie forest, and decided to return home to warm himself near logs of fire in the hut. She would then make lukewarm water and massage every inch of his body and also poured oil on him, as lay beside the logs of fire in the hut. She never believed that Lappia was just playing tricks to see if she would have been bold enough to invite one of the young men in the village to come to sleep with her in his hut, during his absence."

The huge crowd of reapers and onlookers lauded *Yamba* and, with their songs and encouragement, he was urged to continue his very funny story. He yelled, and the large crowd yelled after him, and he then continued his storytelling cunningly.

"A ferocious tiger attacked and killed the domestic animals and most of their kinsmen in Palama village, which was just three miles from Yilandu. Then, all the chiefs called all their most trusted hunters in the clan together, and urged them to chase and kill the furious beast. Lappia was one of the hunters, and he was called to Chief *Gbekah Kondo's* shed.

"The chief then told him that he was very pleased to see him, and that there was a fierce tiger on the loose, and was moving toward Yilandu. It had already killed lots of domestic animals and even some of their kinsmen. The chief reiterated that it was an expedition fraught with the possibility of disastrous consequences, and they, the chiefs, had decided to call upon their most trusted hunters in the entire clan to hunt the savage beast down.

"Lappia had a craggy handsome face with a generous but sensitive curved mouth, and he said with a fierce conviction, "That animal will be dead by tomorrow."

"This made Chief *Gbekah Kondo* and the elders hush their voices and nodded in benediction. They all cheered for

Lappia. He then begged to leave so that he could hurry home to prepare his hunting satchel. He then explained to his wife about the daring hunting expedition. The chief and his council of elders also assured him that they were going to give him enough gunpowder.

"Oh! Lappia," *Yamba* continued dramatically. He met his wife preparing some meal as she labored to blow the dry wood with her breath just for the fire to blaze. He stood beside her and breathed heavily, pretending to be nodding with firmly closed eyes, and rocking his head as if sleep wanted to hammer him into unconsciousness. He cleared his voice and smiled a smile, which wasn't a good sign. He contorted his face as if he wanted to demonstrate cowardice. Yet, he told Lusuh about the tracking of the wild beast that headed towards Yilandu.

"Many farms were abandoned in those days, and the destructive animals and birds fed on the rice at their will and convenience. Tears streamed down his face for leaving Lusuh behind; as he thought that any handsome youth that had previously eyed his beautiful wife would surely have heard about the long and fateful mission. It was therefore a good time to take chance to convince Lusuh that her husband had gone, and was not to return soon. Lappia sat on a wooden stool and rested his back on the wall of the mud hut and started packing his hunting kit and his gun.

"How long are you going away, Lappia?" she questioned him with a cheerful grin on her face.

"Hum, Lusuh, I don't actually know yet, but you will be sleeping in this hut with Sokeh, who is my neighbor's second wife, and your little sister Surnah. I have already made the arrangements," he said.

"While they were in the midst of the discussion, Tambelleh, the chief's emissary, bumped into them and told Lappia that the other hunters anxiously awaited his presence at the chief's shed. He then hurriedly took a few morsels of rice, ate hastily, and bade Lusuh farewell as tears welled in his eyes for leaving his beautiful wife behind.

"Goodbye, Lusuh."

"Goodbye and good luck, my love. May God guide you during that dangerous mission," she said. "I promise to be a good wife in your absence," she added with a contented face and courteous manner.

"The wives consoled the other hunters, who had sat in the chief's shed. Lappia hurriedly left, and Lusuh quickly glanced at him marching away like a giant. Beside the chief's shed the hunters' wives and children and kinsmen stood speechless. There were now no farewells, and no smiles. They all looked at each other while some of the children yelled for their fathers, falling constantly on the dusty ground, and kicking their legs up in the air. The situation was unbearable and poignant. The hunters couldn't look back, according to their custom.

"Some of the elders accompanied them to a considerable distance on the outskirts of the village where they stopped. There they poured gin on the ground, and prayed on a few kola nuts and recited a mysterious incantation as a libation to their great forebears and the gods to guide the hunters during the dangerous mission. After this, the elders stood, and the hunters disappeared on the contoured dusty footpath that led toward the forest. The elders then returned to the village."

Yamba yearned again, and the crowd echoed. The traditional musical instruments played nonstop music, especially when their illustrious and most gifted griot was narrating his very funny story. The mild dancing continued, and the palm and bamboo wine was in abundance. An eagle circled above them in the sky and a toucan cried incessantly on a distant tree.

Yamba could interpret all the signs of the cries of the birds. After taking a few sips of the *Tamba Nanjahn* gin, he continued his story amid the thundering of the talking drums, the shakers and the *KaeNdeh*.

"The hunters knew a secret place in the deep forest where they all gathered, and there they poured a libation and each of them had some idols in their possession. All the other hunters had now joined them. Bopleh the chief hunter again called all of them together. He cautioned them to be very quiet and to only whistle as he demonstrated the sound to them. He then picked some herbs and poured some sacred ointment on them, recited a mysterious incantation. The herb was to make them invisible. He rubbed it on their faces, hands and legs. They were altogether twenty in number. They were all wonderful men, energetic and strong. Only Bopleh and Kepah were old men among them, and they served as powerful men who had mastered the rudiments of forest protection.

"After the ceremony they all remained invisible in the forest. Only they could see each other, but no evil or ferocious animals could see them. They shared their gunpowder. Their guns were loaded by putting long iron rods through the mouths of the ancient guns, until the gunpowder was completely loaded and ready to be fired. They wore hunting charms in the form of sacred shirts made of cotton threads, on which hung different types of idols. This made the hunters armored. It was indeed a very fearful sight to see in those days. They could even kill an elephant when they were in that mood. They then searched the forest but couldn't find the wild animal they tried to kill," *Yamba* echoed again.

The crowd answered in unison and he continued:

"Tiny clouds of yellow and black spotted butterflies circled above their heads. They saw the vipers, boa constrictors, and other poisonous pests, but they couldn't shoot to kill them because they knew that the sound would have alerted the beast. They could see the red streaked sky and the darkness of the night snuffing out the surrounding mountains. Deep in the vast forest surrounding Palama village, they made their camps and rested every night. Monkeys made taunting gestures at them, but the hunters couldn't shoot. It was during one of those nights that Lappia dreamt of his wife, and he woke up abruptly.

"In the dark, eerie and very fearful night, he decided to return to Yilandu to see if his wife had kept her promise. He had surreptitiously slipped out when the other hunters had gone sound asleep and took his loaded gun and jumped into the dark forest. Knowing the footpath very, he reached the outskirts of Yilandu in the very early hours, yet in pitch darkness. Dogs barked angrily at him, and the cats purred continuously. However, he reached the door of his hut. He then looked through a chink and saw someone inside. He knew that it wasn't his wife, and knocked on the door heavily and waited. There wasn't any response.

"He knocked continuously, but Lusuh feared to open the door because she had Tosah, one of the handsome young men of the village, inside. Lappia had had lots of altercations with him, and had openly told him to leave his wife alone. The continuous banging frightened them in the mud hut. Tosah then very frightened, slipped under the bed where he lay comfortably and Lusuh finally opened the door in a very frightened manner. Lappia's gun was aimed in a shooting position when he finally entered into the hut. She could see the devilish manner in him. He was in a fighting mood and she could see vengeance in his eyes," *Yamba* said delightfully.

The enchanting story he was narrating made the reapers on both farms laugh hysterically. Others laughed until they rolled on the ground because his stories were very meaningful and amusing.

"Lusuh laughed sadly but pretended that she was only fooling Lappia to believe that she was with someone inside. She never expected him to know exactly what had taken place in the hut. She had perfectly tied her boyfriend in a large mat, and pushed him under the bed. Lappia then nodded. He sat on a wooden stool and continued to hold his gun in the same position. It was a very fearful sight to see. Lusuh could see a very baleful look on his face. It was then that she knew that she was in trouble.

"Why did you come so soon, Lappia?" she questioned him in surprise and shrugged.

"Don't ask me that stupid question!" he roared back at

her. "Please keep your small mouth shut, or else, you are going to get yours soon!" he bellowed again in trembling anger.

"I have some boiled yams in the calabash. Won't you eat something?" she questioned him quietly and respectfully in her sweet voice.

"I will not eating anything. I told you to close your small mouth," he said angrily.

"Aren't you going to lay your gun down?" she again questioned him sadly.

"No!" he yelled with a very scolding boldness.

"She finally cried and shivered uncontrollably.

"There was another knock on the door, and the jealous hunter rushed and stood behind it. He held his gun firmly as if he were about to shoot at any moment. His wife then sat down and cried bitterly. She continued to bow her head in sadness and disgrace.

"Lappia, slowly opened the door, and Soni, another young man, entered. He was greatly surprised when he saw Lappia instead of Lusuh, and the door slammed violently behind him. He then saw a gun aimed at him. He urinated uncontrollably in his trousers, and every inch of his body was drenched profusely in sweat. He raised his hands as if he was a captured prisoner of war. He cried in deep sorrow and begged for forgiveness. Lappia wouldn't listen to any of his pleas," *Yamba* said emotionally.

The reapers yelled, and the drummers continued to play and others danced. The wonderful reapers enjoyed every bit of it, and the entertaining griot continued to regale them with his very funny story.

"What did you come to do in the very early hours of the morning in my hut?" the outraged husband yelled at the young man.

"Oh! God," exclaimed Soni. "I beg you, Lappia. Don't kill me. Please! Please! Lappia, don't kill me!" he cried continuously. "I only came to beg for fire to light my pipe," he said in his deepest sorrow.

"To light what?" Lappia said.

"A pipe, Oh! My God help me."

"Hey! Lusuh, give him my big tobacco box so that he can smoke his guts out since my hut is the only place in the entire village he had found to be a suitable venue to light his pipe at such an eerie hour of the morning. You stupid fool. I will teach all of you – fools, in this village a good lesson in my hut today," he said in annoyance.

Soni obeyed his orders. He crawled on the bare ground and a bunch of tobacco leaves were ignited and he was forced to smoke to death.

"Hey! Smoke your lungs out. Smoke everything, you stupid fool," Lappia yelled. "You are the most notorious smoker in Yilandu, who disturbs others even during the eerie hours of the morning just to light a pipe," the jealous man growled and hissed at him scornfully, and even spat in his face.

"There the poor young man sat and inhaled clouds of very black smoke into his young lungs. Lappia only made derisive laughter at him. He also pointed his gun at him at a very close range and continued to force him to smoke all the wads of tobacco leaves Lusuh had given to Soni.

"Lusuh then sat sorrowfully and sobbed incessantly.

Lappia had managed to draw Tosah, the first young man, who had wrapped himself inside a large mat, from under the bed, and made him into a seating stool. He sat on him so hard that he cried in great pain," said *Yamba* empathetically.

The huge crowd of reapers, helpers, and dancers roared, "Osieh!" (Hurrah!), and they all answered in unison again, "Eeeeeh!" and died down to allow *Yamba* to continue with his funny story.

"There was another knock on the door, as the guard dogs barked loudly. Lappia again slipped behind the door gently. He pointed his gun at another intruder. He referred to all of them as troublemakers in the village, whose duty was to chase others' wives. He saw another figure in front of him.

"Oh no! It's you, Manfoh. You insulted me on a series of occasions for my wife, and today you have fallen in my trap," he roared, and pointed his gun directly at his head.

"Manfoh raised both hands upright and begged for forgiveness.

""You idiot. Who do you think you are? What made you come this very early in the morning to see my wife?" Lappia said very angrily.

""Eh! Lappia, I felt too hot in my hut, and I only came to cool myself outdoors," Manfoh said hesitantly and clumsily. His hands remained raised in the air as if he was another prisoner of war, caught by the mighty Lappia.

"What! To keep yourself cold? Hey! Lusuh, take that calabash of water and pour it all on his head since he is feeling so hot this very early hour in the morning. This will also help him to feel chilly."

The reapers and the crowd of onlookers who continued to listen to *Yamba*'s very funny story couldn't help laughing. They all praised him. He was indeed an old man who was very gifted in narrating ancient tales, myths, and legends. He was indeed the best storyteller in the Clan. After all the eulogies, he continued with his storytelling after sipping the *Tamba Nanjahn* gin, which he always carried with him in a small bottle, neatly hidden in the many pockets of his country-cloth gown, he then continued:

Lappia continued to punish his prisoners who were guilty of chasing his wife. When the first calabash of water was poured on his head, Manfoh sat down on the muddy floor sadly and cried sadly in Lusuh's name, thus making Lappia more agitated. Manfoh looked around him and saw Soni who had been captured earlier. There he sat gulping unnecessary clouds of a very black smoke into his poor lungs.

"Oh, Lusuh, you have betrayed us," all of them cried sorrowfully.

"Don't call my wife's name, you are all stupid fools. Don't you know that she is a married woman in the village?" Lappia questioned angrily.

"They were now at the mercy of the most jealous man on earth.

"Lappia told Lusuh to continue pouring water on Manfoh's head with very harsh commands. Tosah, the first intruder who had hidden, wrapped up in the mat, also suffered a lot. Lappia sat on him constantly with his fat butt, and he cried in sorrowful pain like a child, since he couldn't bear Lappia's weight who continued to sit all over him as if he was a sack of cleaned rice. Lappia was a fat man with a bulging stomach, which was the result of his constant drinking the palm wine and bamboo wine.

"Tosah suffered massive injuries all over his body. His hands were tied in the mat and he couldn't move to free himself. His pains were more severe than the other prisoners kept by Lappia in his hut. There, Tosah lay and cried in the anguish of severe pain like a baby. Lappia couldn't forgive them. As Soni continued his chain-smoking game, Lusuh continued to pour water on Manfoh's head, while Tosah cried hysterically.

"As the crying continued in the very early hours in the morning, the fowls started to declare daylight with their noises. The distant frogs and toads played drumming tunes too. The ugly voices of the intruders or prisoners in Lappia's hut were now audible.

Bandabellah, an old man, whose hut was closer to Lappia's, heard the noises and the incessant cries. He then woke, and slowly opened the door of his hut. He went to Lappia's hut and slowly knocked at the door. Lappia thought that it was another intruder, and he gently opened the door as usual. It was to his greatest surprise that he saw the old man, who stood in front of him and asked him what was happening in his hut?

"Ah! Ha! I used to tell all of you in the village to tell your sons to leave my wife alone. They ignored all my warnings. They are all intruders who did not see any woman in this village but my wife, Lusuh. Today, I have caught all of them red-handed."

"Lusuh tied her head tie in a Moslem prayer style, and then closed her eyes because of the very shameful act that was surely going to tarnish not only her image, but also that of her entire family in the clan. Old man Bandabellah then begged Lappia who was so furious and continued to stand with his gun, aiming it at all the intruders who were now his prisoners, to carry the matter to the chief's shed. The hunter agreed, and by then, the entire village had woken, and heard how the entire episode had unfolded. Many of the villagers went to the chief's shed.

"Many of them shook their heads incredibly. They all felt that the victims had actually wronged Lappia. Some even suggested that they were very lucky because he could have killed all of them. They were accused of dismantling marriages in the village. Lusuh continued to sit in discontent. She bowed her head in total disgrace. She was caught in the web of her promiscuous escapades. Yet, she was loved dearly by Lappia. The villagers begged him to forgive her, as the young men too begged for forgiveness. They also agreed to respect Lappia and his wife from that very day.

"Lappia then left his wife in the chief's care, and returned to rejoin the other hunters in the forest. He explained to them about what had taken place in Yilandu, and they joked over it for a couple of days. That was how Lappia finally got control of his wife," Yamba said with an abrupt pause.

The huge crowd echoed again, and the songs and drummers joined the festivities again. Then he continued, "After the hunters had slept three nights in the forest, the wild animal was spotted at a stream where it had gone to drink some water. The hunters had technically followed its paw prints in the muddy ground. There they met it, and killed it without any fight. There was great relief in the clan, and the farmers returned to their farms. The hunters were praised for their bravery in the clan."

"Ah! Lappia, he never lived long to see this day," *Yamba* echoed.

Every one cheered for him. He sang, and drummers played tunes to most of his short and very interesting songs. He shook the tail of an unknown animal in his right hand and he sang reggae epics.

The reapers continued with their job, nodding their heads accordingly with content faces. These were the joyous days in Kissi land. The reapers also tied to their hands and below their knees, special amulets in the forms of special idols, which were considered charms. They shook their heads and danced and at the same time did the work energetically. The Ngufueyoh Reapers are still found in the Kissi land to this day.

These reapers also follow laws, which are hidden from outsiders. One can only know them if one is a member of this very mysterious reapers club among the Kissi.

All at once on the chief's farm, a deadly viper bit Chokah who had gone to search for bush rats in an anthill. His friends ran quickly and informed Chief *Gbekah Kondo*.

Tamba Kolloh was summoned immediately. He picked some leaves, and with an ointment he had taken from his satchel, he read a mysterious incantation on the smashed leaves. He then took the *mossoh*, the traditional medication that cured snakebite instantly, and with the smashed leaves, rubbed it on the spot the snake had bitten the little boy. He also pricked some small holes around the same spot and black blood oozed in tiny specks. He then sucked the poison out of his leg. After this, he rubbed the *mossoh* around it and the pain vanished immediately and Chokak was relieved. The work couldn't stop on the farms since snakebite was considered a minor issue in the Kissi culture. They had very effective charms to cure such trifling illnesses.

Tamba Kolloh was also hailed as the only savior in their clan. It was believed that he was indeed a reincarnation of his great grandfather Bandakillie Fugbu who lived in Yilandu many years ago, and who was also a famous deity in Toli. Others hailed him to have obtained such mystic powers from the late Nyuma Mongor, also a famous deity.

The activities had gone pretty well throughout the day on the farms. Darkness was now setting in. The two farms were successfully harvested. The children, women and men transported the loads of the harvested rice on their heads to the village. They made numerous trips. The children roasted the stalks of corn they had collected on the farm. The dancers and reapers danced their way from the farms until they entered into the village.

That evening, Chief *Gbekah Kondo* and the elders were so happy that they entertained the reapers and they danced until the wee hours of the morning. *Yamba*'s voice was still heard the next day. The harvested rice was neatly packed in the huge barns in the village. There were also many kegs of palm and bamboo wine in the chief's shed. They had a very good harvest in Yilandu that season.

Outdoor Activities in Yilandu

Yilandu was blessed to have had lots of outdoor activities enjoyed by elders, chiefs, and even the ordinary inhabitants in the village. Wrestling was among one of the most thrilling and anxiously awaited game that kept them busy, and they enjoyed the cool zephyrs of the evenings. The game brought not only Yilandu, but the entire Toli clan together.

They called wrestling ***Nken-dun-ngbe*-deh** or ***Le-gbedon-kaen-doh***. It metaphorically means "to make the ribs strong." Such contests were organized by the strongest men or the chiefs and elders in the village, and the purpose was to make the weaker men physically strong and to get them ready for war if that was the case. It should be noted that "*chovoh*" means war, and "*chea-la-bar*" means to fight.

In order to make two enemies or friends fight, there were men who instigated them by pulling hairs on their heads. The person, who goes to pull hairs on the head on an opponent, will then start the fight. If that did not work, the stronger man will pretend to touch another man's crotch, which symbolized an undignified attitude and disgrace in the Kissi culture, and thus a fight may be provoked.

It should be clear that stronger men wore amulets and other idols which were made by the native herbalists and they used them to make them invincible, stronger, and more protected. On important wrestling days, traditional musicians and griots were invited, and the drummers and shaker players, and women with melodious voices sang and played nonstop. The tapers brought enough palm and bamboo wine, and the locally distilled cane juice, or *Tamba Nanjah*n, was in abundance for everyone to enjoy.

Yamba Yilandu the most prolific of all griots in the clan, sat at a vantage point, and narrated the ebullient songs of old, and how their audacious warriors like Gbekah Kondo and Bandakille Fugbu, who lived in Yilandu at that time. Also, were Bundo Kevoh who lived at Turadu village; Kpangolo, who lived in Fendu village; Konoh who lived in Chaesenei; and the famous Bundo Nyumodu of Nyumodu village. Their exploits were legendary and defied human bravery, and they were considered gods of their time. They fought wars as far as in parts of today's Liberia and in Guinea.

The stronger man who pinned four guys down was considered a hero and would then become an elder, headhunter, marry, and have children and be given land by the chiefs to lay farms; and would be a leader in war. The ground was prepared in such a way that it was like a mat, made with grass they cut from the swamp which appeared like a sponge so that anyone who fell would be protected from injuries.

The fight was conducted in a manner where the contestants did not intend to hurt each other. There was mild kicking and mild fist fighting and swinging, but the main aim was to pin someone down and hold them until they voiced out openly that they have been defeated. They fought many times, and a person has to be defeated four times before winner could be crowned the victor.

Such extravaganzas were held after the farming season, when the rains had ceased and the ground was hard, and the Kissi had enough food, they ate during these occasions. Yet, the griots were the praise singers who constant reported the results of the wrestling match, and announced who was victim, and who was victor.

The occasion was blessed when the moon light showered them with rays of beams, and the singers sang incessantly, the drums echoed nonstop, and Yamba Yilandu, the legendary griot, yelled constantly, to keep the peace.

CHAPTER FIVE

By now, Tamba Kolloh's fame had gone far and wide. He was the most renowned psychic, herbalist, and witch doctor in the clan. The death of Nyuma Mongor had sent an invitation to the wicked witches to go wild with their sorcery—targeting mostly innocent babies and children. They bewitched even adults, who got sick and lay very helpless, barely able to open their eyes; they died of protracted illnesses in the webs of very mysterious circumstances. The innocent children were so enchanted by the acts of the witches that death was always the end result of their curiosity.

The chiefs and the elders consulted with Tamba Kolloh, and asked him to go on a witch-hunt in all villages on the clan. It was launched to root out the very ruthless evil doers. He was now the highest chief priest in the clan. All the idols were under his control, even the ones the most evil men used to hurt others.

Some of the witches who suspected the immensity of Tamba's mystic powers secretly ran to his hut in a steady stream, and bowed and begged deeply in a plea for forgiveness. Many of them felt that he was a young man, and that he had become very obnoxious and stubborn recently in his action to prove that he was now the most dynamic psychic in the clan, and so, they should challenge his power.

The history of the clan was loaded with sorcery, and the very ill and innocent that had lost loved ones to such sinister behavior now prayed that Tamba Kolloh would wage vengeance on their behalf. They believed that he was now the only individual who had that knife of authority.

The chiefs and elders met constantly in the shed to discuss the evil epidemic that had blown like a gale in the clan, all mounted against the youthful generation. The elders' eyes were almost black with an impersonal hatred for the so-called witches, and they believed that crushing them was now the most appropriate solution to their problem.

"Take Dundoh's little daughter, for instance," said Saki who sat with his eyes brimming with sadness. "A pretty little girl that was playing around in the village the other day lay dead in an instant, without any protracted illness, a few days ago. Yawah, as she was called, lay in the grave with eyes wide open, as if she looked keenly at those who had killed her," he concluded pathetically.

"What about Focko's eldest son," said Sakillah, "who was struck on the head by someone who had nursed a dragon in the village? He died slowly in his sleep on the farm."

"Did you hear about the death of Kpakah's bouncing baby boy who was playing around on the farm just a week ago?" said Kumba. "He asked his mother to suckle her breast. He was fed. He grew stiff, stretched his hands and feet and died instantly. It was widely believed that a dragon that knocked him on the head the same day also caused his death. I was on the farm, and I saw a very horrible death for an infant of that age," Kumba added sadly.

Chief *Gbekah* called the entire village together. He

disclosed to them that, "the entire clan was swept by death, which was a very hideous and a colossal effrontery perpetuated by their own very insane and wicked kinsmen. They had succumbed to sorcery and were thus murdering innocent children in large numbers like an epidemic across the clan."

In the midst of the gathering, Finda, an energetic nursing mother, entered with loosed hair and fell down on the muddy floor in the shed. She kicked her legs in the air and cried as if in the anguish of great pain.

"Oh! Chief *Gbekah*! My little son is unconscious and at the point of death. He had just suffered from a trifling cold last night, but has grown severe today," she cried haggardly and lay at the chief's feet.

The elders held her. They consoled her and immediately sent for Tamba Kolloh. He came in seconds with his satchel, performed some mysterious signs with medicinal herbs, and immediately restored the little boy's health and life.

Finda then felt at ease and thanked the elders, and especially Tamba Kolloh, who had tied a special idol in the form of an amulet that represented the god of good health, around the little boy's neck. He then rubbed a black liquid on every inch of his body, thus anointing him against human sorcery. He was one of the very lucky ones, who were cured by Tamba Kolloh's mystic ointments and herbs. Immediately upon reaching home with his mother, he felt comfortable and slept very well.

The elders then held an impromptu meeting in which they unanimously agreed to launch a witch hunt. Tamba

Kolloh was then called to the meeting. He was informed about the very terrible situation they faced not only in Yilandu, but the entire clan. It had caused the death of hundreds of their loved ones, and he was now given the authority to destroy all the human vampires, witches, and those who nursed dragons in the clan. They then boasted of his very effective psychic powers which they said he had acquired from his forebears whose countless victories over such wicked crimes were never mere bluff, but a genuine mystic inheritance deeply rooted in the ancient gods of the clan, whose idols were still alive and smiling.

Decibels of murmur competed with the degrees of heat as hot sweat dripped off the elder's faces under the chief's thatched roof shed. Although they enjoyed some ventilation on some days, others, the heat of the tropical sun sometimes became unbearable, even causing a downpour of showers in the day. Yet today, the cool air managed to blow until it gained the upper hand.

Tamba Kolloh had long awaited this privilege. He now developed an animal instinct for danger and continued to be tinged with the continuous pleas from the venerable elders and innocent villagers to defend them from the human cannibals who only waged war on innocent and unarmed children.

It was just after the harvest season and the rains had set in. All the inhabitants of the village were now indoors because of the intermittent rainfall during the rainy season. Some, though, went to their old farmland, to collect vegetables and plant yams, cassavas and other crops. The witch hunt could then be properly launched in the village.

It was one evening when most of the villagers had returned from their chores that *Yamba*'s voice was heard again, "To the sons, daughters and all the elders of our village, I have an important message to convey to all of you from your chief and his elders. They had assembled and had discussed in detail about the evil acts committed against our children and our loved ones. It's therefore in this respect that our most superb and mystic witch doctor, Tamba Kolloh, will be displaying his most gifted and supernatural talents to weed out the culprits.

"They have asked that the witch hunt be launched tomorrow and it is expected to last for two days. The elders have asked that everyone participates, and that anyone absent on these days will be considered a suspect and culprit in such crimes. Every hut's door that will be marked with a charcoal will be considered suspicious," he cried in every corner in the village.

The dogs didn't bark at him much, since they were now accustomed to his constant cries. Yet some of them barked once or twice. The cats purred and the cocks crowed when he passed between the huts and called out near them. The cows mooed and goats bleated intermittently though the dirty pigs lay unconcerned in the mud.

That evening, the village grew extremely dull and quiet. Tamba Kolloh was the first witch hunter to dance in Yilandu. It was indeed going to commence an eerie and a spine-chilling adventure, which was surely going to cost many lives. That night, *Yamba's* voice echoed in the village as an invincible flight of insects, the entire village appeared to be very lonesome, though it was deserted.

Yet in Tamba Kolloh's hut, a steady stream of evil men and women with strange devilish faces, appeared, showing an evil element, which disappeared as quickly as it had come, when they approached the most deadly and very powerful idols in his den. Tamba Kolloh was now considered the most fearsome juju man and even the most gifted deity in the clan.

Kumba Mongor now greatly assisted him. The villagers soon discovered that she was as gifted as Tamba Kolloh was in such cultural powers. Since she and Tamba were not yet married, they still lived in their separate homes. However, she came around to assist him in case he needed her assistance.

In Tamba Kolloh's hut, to reiterate, there were idols of various sizes and of different spiritual powers. There were huge amulets that hung grotesquely from the thatched roof ceiling, many others hung on the mud wall. There were also many clay pots of various sizes that contained exotic herbs in liquids forming an emollient substance, which produced foam even without heating them over fire.

At the door hung a sacred bottle in which was also an exotic liquid that also foamed with a flush of scum inside. It was to kill anyone who entered into his room with any evil intention. Also, invisible in the den were poisonous and deadly serpents in the form of huge boas, cobras, and vipers that were sent on special missions to pick sacred herbs to cure those who were very sick and had been brought to his hut to be healed.

At certain instances, nocturnal animals and insects called out loudly in the darkness of the hut. Rats scurried in and out of their holes, and, in the midst of all that, strange faces continued to enter into Tamba's room, pleading for forgiveness.

Tamba sat and listened keenly to accounts of infamous exploits and vicious acts, but vowed never to pardon them again if they were to engage in such evil acts in the village. He only nodded his head gently and even joked that it wasn't any time to indulge in long explanations, since he knew all of them in the entire clan.

Tamba then begged them to let him take just a few hours of rest, since he was to commence his job the next day. He was still awake when the cocks started crowing and the toads and frogs in the distant swamps started drumming tunes. For the witches in the clan, he was their most vicious enemy. He was going to abolish the awful and unspeakable acts in the clan. Tamba Kolloh's name smelt badly in their noses and created great fear in them all—he lay in his impregnable den with a spiritual and mystic omnipotence.

Early the next day when most of the villagers were still in bed and planning the day's activities, Tamba Kolloh went to feed the idols at his shrine, under the kola nut tree. There he met the ghost of Nyuma Mongor, and Tamba was bathed with more sacred liquids and ointments. He was then given supreme powers and was told never to be afraid of anyone in the clan, but to proceed on a violent witch-hunt. The gods of his forebears were now guiding him in the clan against all human evils.

It was also under the same kola nut tree that he heard *Yamba* echoing his final message in the village:

"Today is the day we have all awaited. Everyone should

remain in their huts," yelled the griot. "Our son Tamba Kolloh, now our most famous chief priest, will perform prodigiously with his supernatural powers. He has been asked to adopt this hunt with speed, and an inflexible firmness of purpose, valor, stamina and great intelligence, his cause of action. Today is the day. The destruction of any innocent life is a great crime on earth."

Yamba took a deep breath and relaxed slightly. He marched like a giant as he heavily limped on one leg. He went to Tamba Kolloh's hut and echoed a few eulogies. Tamba Kolloh had just left the kola nut tree where he had performed the most appropriate rituals, and calling upon the gods of his forebears to guide him against all odds and any misfortunes or challenges that could have debarred him from any successes during the witch-hunt in Yilandu.

The idols stood and smiled. Then exotic ointments were poured on them. It was then that they became lively. *Yamba* yelled:

"Oh! Tamba Kolloh, the warrior of warriors, and the great grandson of Bandakillie Fugbu of Yilandu, a warrior whose shots are the most accurate and very fatal in the clan: Your power will ever be remembered in the annals of the history of Toli. For if any man beats rice flower in a mortar with a pestle and boasts that his girlfriend did it for him; well, it's his own business, and it's left to him to decide. If you are not a sorcerer or witch, rest assured that Tamba Kolloh's armor shall pass over you.

"If you pretend and you are caught, you will surely face the consequences of his amour. Oh! The days of Nyuma Mongor, if he were alive today, he should have performed this ceremony with absolute authority too. Nyuma Mongor was indeed a tiger, the boa, and the lion of Toli. The witches were afraid of him," *Yamba* said as he walked toward Tamba Kolloh's hut.

There he was offered some *Tamba Nanjah*n gin and few kola nuts for his good work informing the villagers about the ceremony.

Tamba Kolloh had already dressed in his magic shirt, which was neatly made of cotton threads on which were hung all types of amulets, and all sizes of bottles tied to it. He also had on his head a mystic hat decorated with shells of different colors and different sizes. He was now the servant of Gbulamah (god of truth and justice). He had the idol that signified that god too.

In his hand was a very strange tail of an unknown animal, which he shook and danced with to the rhythms of the talking-drums. The drummers and the few dancers were called, and the occasion was graced by the presence of the chief and his most trusted and venerable elders. Some came from distant villages in the clan. They all sat comfortably in the chief's shed. They discussed the power that they had given Tamba Kolloh to exercise on the very ruthless men and women who had engaged in such evil acts; a very sharp knife of authority.

Those who had lost loved ones made their last impulsive gestures by kneeling at the chief's feet, and they vowed to avenge the mysterious deaths of their children.

Yet, Tamba Kolloh had not appeared. He was still in consultation with the charms. He understood what action was most appropriate to take in such life and death situations. Kumba Mongor had already lost five moons and so, she couldn't help in the witch hunt, which was done with hectic exercise and required running around in a very frantic mood, from hut to hut. The hunt also involved a massive display of energy and excessive strength, especially when Tamba had to carry a specially made mystic sword, which he also used as a charm.

A huge crowd had gathered in the village, all earnestly expected Tamba. The youthful generation that had already admired such boldness praised him, and also considered him to be their savior. He had cured them from constant snakebites and saved them from the claws of instant death. Even their neighbors from distant villages came in a steady stream, some eager to see a witch hunt for the first time in their lives.

The drums echoed as *Yamba* yelled. The elders rigidly kept their eulogies and rites sacred. They also felt it necessary to keep up some semblance of dignity, assuming an air of mystery, and they gave everything a nebulous significance.

What Tamba had been asked to demonstrate on that day was knowledge, which had been transmitted to him by the ancient deities in the clan, and especially in the families in which they had lived. They knew that he wasn't someone who offered vague and nebulous assertions none of which could be proven; but a man who gave a clear, reasonable, convincing moral explanation of any mystery he was obliged to elucidate.

The rivers and streams also gave the Kissi mystic powers, and they received their children through prayers and sacrifices they made on their banks.

As the sun was just about to stand erect in the azure sky, Tamba stepped out gigantically and went straight to the chief's shed with his mystic sword in his right hand and the mysterious tail in his left hand. No one knew exactly from where he got the sword and the tail. It was just the sign of the ruthlessness of the game that lay ahead in the day.

The talking drums played nonstop music. The tunes were very strange too. The musicians played tunes for special ceremonies. Yet, the tunes played that day were so strange that no one could decipher their meaning.

Yamba at certain instances raised his voice to the highest pitch. He narrated stories of the legendary Bandakillie Fugbu of Yilandu, who, as he narrated, was also one of the greatest men that ever lived in the clan. He reported that Bandakillie in his day called out huge boa constrictors from the forest around Yilandu, narrating sacred incantations to them in the village during broad daylight. These creatures gave him messages from the dead or from some aliens from distant planets.

Bandakillie alone tied baboons on Ngebadu; even talked to them. He performed lots of wonders that were never written but remained narrated in the oral traditions of the Kissi.

The women who had lost their babies to such vicious acts of witchcraft prostrated themselves at Tamba Kolloh's feet and begged him not to hide anyone who was considered an enemy of the babies, for the good of the clan. Tamba Kolloh then stood speechless; his body was drenched with perspiration. He was greatly admired by his kinsmen.

It was in the midst of the clamor that *Yamba* echoed for silence and Chief *Gbekah Kondo* stood up. He slowly gathered the huge arms of his country-cloth gown and boldly said:

"My kinsmen, there has been a deadly epidemic that has swept across our village and even the clan. Our babies and loved ones have suffered most awfully at the hands of some people who have waged a relentless war on the innocent—most of whom have succumbed to their terror, and died mysteriously. It's therefore with the consent of the elders in Yilandu and in the clan that we have asked our son Tamba Kolloh to launch a witch hunt."

The entire crowd that had gathered cheered for him and all agreed with a big, "EEeeh!"

Yamba then yelled an ancient verse and died down slowly to allow Chief Gbekah to carry on with his very historic and powerful speech.

"My kinsmen," continued the chief. "We will again live wonderful, exciting, and glamorous lives so long as the impostures who have indulged in such infamous acts be weeded out once and for all."

The crowd cheered for him again. There was now dancing and crying in some corners in the village. Some cried for their loved ones who had died mysteriously in the village. The talking-drums played.

Yamba again echoed, "Ouh! Ouh! Ouh!" and there was silence again to allow the chief to continue.

"Therefore, in my capacity as Chief of Yilandu, and also as a venerable elder in the Toli Clan it is my patriotic duty, my fellow kinsmen, to now authorize Tamba Kolloh to go on a very wild and violent witch-hunting spree in vengeance. He should catch the culprits and bring them to justice," said the chief in great admonishment. "We want to know what the innocent children have done. Let's not hide them. Even those who nurse dragons in the village, and hid idols, should be shown in public today. It's so deplorable to allow such insidious practices in our midst."

The chief paused and the villagers roared in agreement.

"Oh! Tamba Kolloh," he continued. "Demonstrate the virtues of loyalty, courage and truthfulness of character. The entire village is now in your hands. Rule it with absolute authority!" Chief *Gbekah Kondo* concluded with a fierce conviction.

Kendema, a venerable elder in Yilandu echoed, "Osieh!"

It was a warrior's cry, and the large crowd answered "E*Eeeh*!"

Tears continued to stream down the faces of all those who had gathered and the drummers echoed with their very tuneful, ancient lyrics, suitable for such an occasion. They sang and played behind Tamba Kolloh. *Yamba* also accompanied them from hut to hut in the village.

In the middle of the village was an open space where he, Tamba Kolloh, neatly placed a huge idol of *Sangah* (god of punishment and death). It was a huge structure wrapped in a white country-cloth, and no one knew exactly how it was made. Yet, the spot at which the idol lay was where the culprits were to line up and await their judgment. He pointed his mysterious sword at the spot in a dancing mood.

There the witches would sit in the hot burning sun. The object was considered a magnetic snare that attracted evil men to it with great force. Most of them were forcefully dragged to it. There were bruises on their bodies. When the actual witch hunt commenced, Tamba Kolloh never spoke to anyone. He only looked at their faces. Those he suspected were touched with his magic sword in a dancing and rocking mood.

Yamba's voice echoed again in the background. The children were so afraid that they clung to their mothers, who breast-fed them at intervals. The juju men and women who couldn't wait to be disgraced went peacefully to the magnetic snare. Yet, the stubborn ones were dragged mysteriously to it. At certain instances, the magnetic sword was raised in the air as if in a fighting mood.

Tamba Kolloh swung the sword relentlessly, as if at war with many warriors who also fought back boldly just to save their lives. He was a medium-build man, with a heavy weight. On his legs below his ankles were tied mysterious strings with colorful beads and some noisy bangles that shook gigantically when he stepped. On his wrists were also tied the same strings, and he shook them when he danced in a trembling mood. It sent tremors of fear into every heart. The drummers followed him everywhere he went in the village.

During the witch hunt, as Tamba Kolloh swung his magic sword relentlessly, everyone saw fresh blood dripping in the muddy ground as those wounded or killed in witch battle remained invisible. They were considered those who challenged Tamba Kolloh's armor, and he had no choice but to destroy them.

He then boasted, "Some people had challenged him, but that he had to destroy them."

Such culprits remained alive in the village, but later died under some mysterious circumstances a few days after the witch-hunt. Burials for such evil men and women were held occasionally in the village. The crowd then cheered for Tamba Kolloh.

Yamba lauded him for his bravery. *Kolooh* also joined this historic occasion and it now became lively with much dancing and so much fun. She yelled to the villagers and told them never to challenge Tamba Kolloh in his fight to save the village.

Kooloh could dance extremely well to the sound of the samba and the other traditional instruments. As a village philosopher, her face was always painted with mystic white clay, which demonstrated a special dispensation to the gods of the shrines and the oracles in the clan. She danced as far as to the magnetic structure, and returned in a shaking style perfectly marching the rhythms of the drums that echoed in Yilandu. She was indeed a great performer.

The villagers always loved *Kolooh* and they cheered for her too. She actually shared much fun with them and even to this day, the Kissi always talk about her in their stories.

Dundoh, an old man whose mysterious dragon struck Sindoh's daughter's head, as she was playing on the family farm, was among those who had been dragged to the mysterious spot, and he sat near Sangah, the god of justice and punishment. He had hidden in his hut at first, but Tamba Kolloh reached there and pointed his magic sword at the door. Dundoh was forcefully dragged out as far as to the magnetic snare. In his possession was a large satchel, in which lay a mysterious idol that he could transform into an invisible boa constrictor or into a dragon after he recited some mysterious incantation over it. It could never be seen with the naked eye, except by someone who also had some knowledge of such outrageous and wicked crimes.

Although Sindoh had gone earlier and apologized to Tamba Kolloh for her own actions, yet, the magic sword dragged her to the mysterious spot and there she sat near Sangah. It was for the very first time that such a sacred witch-hunt expedition was held in Yilandu.

Tamba Kolloh wanted to be neutral, and impartial to all the culprits. Now, Sindoh and Dundoh sat beside each other on the muddy ground, and Sindoh accused the old man of trying to kill her daughter on the farm.

The old man told her that they had all been caught red-handed by Tamba Kolloh's supreme and supernatural powers, and that anger and recrimination at that particular point could serve no useful purpose for all of them.

The villagers who stood and watched only booed, and made fun of them. The captives knew that it wasn't any time for unkind and destructive remarks, since all of them had been caught by Tamba Kolloh's supernatural armor.

As the witch hunt progressed and grew more tedious, most of those involved wouldn't come out since they were ashamed. Tamba Kolloh had to enter into the huts, where he pointed his magic sword at them. If the door was neatly closed, he just pointed his magic sword at it, and it opened slowly. Those who remained stubborn and fought back were massacred mysteriously as blood continued to drip from his magic sword.

The huge clouds that had gathered vanished as soon as *Kolooh* had appeared. No one knew how she actually held the droplets of rainfall during any important occasion in the village. The rain producing clouds gave way to a bright blue sky, and lovebirds and butterflies were again seen all over as they flew very low on the heads of the onlookers who gently brushed the butterflies away.

The center of the village was now overcrowded. People came from distant villages to see what Tamba Kolloh was going to do in their village too. They returned home and reported what they saw to the other villagers who couldn't come to Yilandu on that historic day. The drums rose to a frenzy and when the day had long gone, most of the villagers were engaged in the dancing.

Tamba Kolloh then summoned Chief *Gbekah* and his council of elders and presented the witch-hunt prisoners to them. Tamba Kolloh approached the drummers, and he danced and shook his entire body to the rhythms of the drums. He still had his magic sword and the mysterious tail in his possession.

Tamba then asked the culprits to confess in the presence of the elders. Yet, according to Kissi norms, confession meant death. The only person who could change things around, and give their lives back was now the witch hunter, Tamba Kolloh. He now had their lives in his magic sword and calling anyone's name and at the same time raising and making a cutting movement, meant instant death to that individual.

Some of them confessed, and begged for forgiveness. Those who had indulged in more heinous crimes were afraid to confess, but Tamba Kolloh definitely told them that without a sincere confession, he was ready to take the law into his hands. His words frightened the culprits, and their actual confessions began, "I'm Sindoh. I have an idol in the form of an amulet left to me by my late grandmother. I have never destroyed any human life although I have bewitched lots of innocent children in Yilandu. I am therefore asking Tamba Kolloh, the chief, elders and my people in the village, to pardon me. I will never indulge in such a wicked act again," she said with tears in her eyes.

Tamba Kolloh nodded, and she was told to sit aside.

"I am Dundoh. I have with me an idol of an invisible dragon, which I have used to strike lots of innocent children and even adults in Yilandu and in other villages where I went on visits over the past years."

The crowd booed noisily at him.

"Hey! Were you the very one who had intended to kill Sindoh's daughter on the farm?" asked an elder.

"Well, I was on the same farm on that day."

"You were the very one, you stupid idiot," yelled Sindoh who was also in the dragnet, having just confessed. She continued to make a baleful countenance at the old man.

"But who knows what all you have done too?" the old man roared back.

"That is not your business. I have confessed already," Sindoh said.

"You should be concerned with all the murders that you have committed," she advised him and stood to slap the old man but she was held down and controlled.

The crowd again booed at them noisily. *Yamba* yelled again for silence. The crowd roared with great excitement and much laughter, the booing continued unabated.

The confessions continued. The onlookers keenly listened while the others shed clouds of tears. The drummers played nonstop music, and *Yamba* echoed every word that was said either by Tamba Kolloh, Chief *Gbekah Kondo*, his elders, and even the culprits. Tamba Kolloh stood like an elephant, with his magic sword in his hand.

Among those who made incredible confessions was an enigmatic and frail old lady called Kumtoh. She had known quite well that she was surely going to die, and so, decided to repent in the presence of her kinsmen and thus asked them for forgiveness. She confessed silently, and *Yamba* echoed every word that came from her mouth.

The huge crowd listened, and *Yamba* continued to echo everything the old woman confessed for those villagers who stood in distant corners in the village to hear.

Tamba Kolloh was again called to undertake the burial of the witches who died after the witch hunt, after reciting a special incantation for the dead, and asking the gods what appropriate steps to take before and even after burial. If the Kissi didn't do it rightly, the dead would appear as vampires in the clan which the Kissi called, *Ngalangafoh (a vampire).* These would appear in one's dreams, and disturb you greatly. They would even go on a spree of death and human destruction. Tamba Kolloh was again hailed as the savior of Toli, he was now reigning—the most famous deity.

In the eerie and dark forests that surrounded the village, owls hooted out loudly and plaintively. Somewhere in the far distance, others answered their cry. There was an intermittent shower.

That night, a huge boa emerged from the forest and crawled into the village. It lay at the door of the mud hut where Kumtoh had lain sick and had died. A relative who had wanted to stand on her legs early that morning opened the door as the moon shone brightly at its zenith in the sky. She abruptly fell on her back and yelled for help. By the time her friends came out doors to see what had frightened her, they only saw the huge boa that was crawling back into the coffee and cacao plantation that surrounded the village.

It was then that they realized that old woman Kumtoh had finally disappeared. The incident was later reported to Chief *Gbekah Kondo* and Tamba Kolloh. It was also reported through the clan. The mud hut was deserted, and no one slept in it again.

After the witch hunt that season, there were lots of burials in Yilandu and in the clan. The villagers now breathed a sigh of relief from their wicked tormentors who had waged a nasty war on their precious lives.

Tamba Kolloh slept one night, and had a dream in which his great grandfather, Bandakillie Fugbu appeared to him. He told Tamba that he had appeared to him to expose more mysteries to him and to teach him more mysterious incantations that could unravel the unexplained secrets to him. He could now play the harp very well. He went to the Pela stream, and played it there. This invited some very strange creatures that divulged more mysteries to him.

Tamba was now regarded as the custodian and the middleman on whom his kinsmen relied to explain to them some unearthly mysteries and how they could contact their loved ones beyond, through his psychic powers. He was the only person who talked to the dead. The younger generation now gained a whole lot and was fortunate to exploit his vast galleries, of supernatural predominance.

Women who couldn't bear children now went to Tamba Kolloh, and he carried them to *Koei*, (*the god of fertility*). Such trips were made to a shrine near the Pela and Boon streams or to a sacred location in a swamp. After the ceremony, the final prayers were said in Tamba's hut, and the young women were told to touch certain idols that stood with children in their dreams. These young women were surely going to bear children.

Among the most powerful but dangerous gods in the possession of such chief priests among the Kissi is called, *Domah,* which can take the form of different types of idols such as: rings, sacred shirts, coins, or any objects that one could hold and keep in their possession. *Domah* makes someone very prominent, very rich, and able to get whatever they may like in this world. It's the most dynamic god that any man can get in contact with even to this day in Kissi land.

Yet there are lots of laws if someone should like to get and keep this god. Any mistake in keeping the laws meant an instant death. Many of the younger generation among the Kissi died under such mysterious circumstances since they overlooked the laws, and even forgot to return to thank the witch-doctor, herbalist, or the chief priest who enabled them to be in contact with the god. The constant obscurity enabled the Kissi to create some fear and a semblance of dignity, which added much mystery to their culture.

Yet no one should be fooled to undertake any trip to get the *Domah* in Kissi land. For any mistakes in keeping any of the laws of this god, may result to some very serious consequences. It's nothing to actually joke with.

Any time Tamba Kolloh was called upon to perform the appropriate ceremonies, the chief, his elders and the villagers wanted to see what mysteries he was going to transmit to them from the forbearers. The village grew eerie, calm and unreal. Silence was only broken by the countless noises of insects, birds, the toads and frogs in the distant swamps. They poured white clay all around the oracles or shrines, and flour was made from rice. It was then made into small balls and placed on leaves with kola nuts, which were sometimes broken in halves. The idols were then decorated with beads of different colors; kola nuts were also placed near them. The flour was rubbed on their faces.

Tamba Kolloh then took a harp and played some mysterious tunes, calling on the names of their ancestors who were considered gods in the clan. It was their inexplicable deeds that propounded the dogma of the spiritual evolution in the clan. Their teachings left a propound imprint on their mental and spiritual achievements of the Kissi.

Yamba, who was sometimes present, also helped in calling the names of the ancient gods since he was very versed in doing so. Even in his hut, Tamba Kolloh could be heard playing his harp when he was ready to enter into the spirit world. Yet, everything remained invisible around him. He could see all the fearful creatures very well. He nodded his head when they spoke with him, and he never stopped playing his harp when he was in that mood.

Everyone who went to see him in his hut for such spiritual blessings only sat calmly and watched in dismay. It was a terrifying experience indeed. They were a sacred sect of people whose ancestors were now considered gods and legends, and were with them. They were always ready to help them as long as they continued to pour libations on them. The Kissi blessed their ancestors with libations, who in turn made their crops productive, they claimed joyously and in an ineffable way.

Other villagers came to Tamba Kolloh for such spiritual guidance and assistance. He gave them special idols to assist them in their everyday endeavors. The oracles and the shrines in Yilandu were always congested with a steady flow of visitors who came to gain from such unbelievable and supernatural gifts around them.

Some brought fowls and other domestic animals to him as payment for the great service he offered to them. Even if he wasn't able to accompany them to the sacred spots, some elders carried the visitors to those indiscernible gods to adore them so they would answer their prayers; at the same time praying to God Almighty, to crown such demands. Their requests were mutually rewarded; they left, praised the gods and told others to come. Yet, they lived their time. They enjoyed the spiritual evolution that befitted their norms and aspirations.

Even Sahr Ponpondo, and his wife Kemah, left Ye*Ndeh* village and came to consult with the spiritual gods of Yilandu. He had wanted his wife to have children but she was barren. They consulted with Tamba Kolloh who advised them to get some basic ointments, shells, a white hen, and some red kola nuts. They came and slept in Yilandu.

Early the next day, they went to Tamba Kolloh's shrine to consult with Koie, the god of fertility. There they killed the hen, and the blood was splattered around the shrine. The kola nuts were neatly placed there on leaves.

Tamba then held the Finda's hands and narrated a mysterious incantation. Her breasts were naked and she tied a newly woven country-cloth around her waist. After he narrated the strange incantation, he smashed some exotic leaves in a calabash and gave the black content to Finda Ponpondo to drink. She was then bathed with the leaves that remained in the calabash, and Tamba Kolloh told her not to bathe again the same day, but the next day.

When they returned to Yilandu, he played his harp, and poured some libations to the living idols. The visitors happily returned to Ye*Ndeh* the next day.

It was just after a few months that they sent word to Tamba Kolloh that she was pregnant. He too sent word to them that after carefully consulting with his shells, Finda Ponpondo was going to have a bouncing baby boy. So it happened, exactly. Such stories are even told to this day in Kissi land.

CHAPTER SIX

Kumba Mongor now grew hefty and bulky, and she couldn't play idly as she did before. She now neared the ninth month of her pregnancy. There were certain things she couldn't eat according to the Kissi culture.

Tamba Kolloh now thought that at his age, young, energetic and versatile, and now a man of great prominence, wealth and pride, he should now officially be in want of a wife.

In the Kissi culture, a woman can stay a concubine, get pregnant, have a child, and at the same time get married. Marriage was just a reunion of the parents of the bride and the bridegroom. The parents of the groom were asked to "*tie-the-kola.*" In some instances, kola nuts were tied in small bundles or put inside a calabash. The elders then presented them to the bride's family in the absence of the groom.

Such consultations continued and were just a step toward the actual marriage. The consultation and the pouring of the libations continued. The "kola" was then "tied" in the bride's home. Money wasn't used in those days. Wealth was based on the amount of domestic animals that a man could produce; and acres of farmland he cultivated. It was the same that determined his prominence in the village.

Gunpowder was also regarded as a sacred item, and was used in most public functions. It was presented to the chiefs as a sign of respect, and also used to drive evil spirits and spells from the village. It was therefore appropriate to note that a dowry or bride price was given in kind. Such was to be counted from the first day that a suitor started offering goods or domestic animals to the bride's family and to the bride herself especially in divorce cases.

In case the bride abandoned the marriage, the native court system in Kissi land undertook the counting of the dowry. It sometimes took months just to finish counting a dowry. It was a very tedious process, and such was usually done during the dry season, after the Kissi reaped their crops on the farms. Some very wicked in-laws requested lots of items, like domestic animals, money which was in the form of a Kissi-penny from the suitor.

Each family kept their valuable domestic animals like goats and cows in corrals, which were just an enclosed place in the village or on the outskirts of the village. Yet the cows and pigs were sometimes left to roam the countryside. In fact, the cows, goats and the dirty pigs were left to roam in the village and dropped their dung everywhere.

Some villagers at leisure found the dung useful as cement, and they rubbed it on the mud walls of their huts. When the dung caked on the walls, it wasn't easy for rodents, insects, and snakes to make holes in the mud wall.

Kpannah Mongor's joy was now tinged with irritation, and she was taking pride in the very young nursing mother her daughter Kumba was soon to be. She also felt elated, since her son-in-law was now the most respectable herbalist chief priest in the clan. He has also kept his promise to marry Kumba Mongor, and he stuck to his promise. Even the villagers could see a sigh of great relief in her eyes in those days.

The Kissi women welcomed the title of a grandmother

with open arms. These grandmothers in the Kissi culture were also the baby-sitters. The families never abandoned their old. They shared fun with them, and there is a saying in the Kissi culture that grandmothers spoil children. They don't eat behind them. Grandchildren never allowed someone to injure their grandmothers—they remained until death. As long as Tamba Kolloh was now engaged to marry Kumba Mongor, both families were to automatically become *Bolah*. It was there that the fun and mischief started in the village.

During the farming season, Tamba Kolloh was now responsible to care for both families. He paid laborers to work on both the Mongor and the Kolloh farms. Even the riches he gathered from the psychic economy and from the displays and cures in the clan were shared with his fiancée's family. He was adored and well paid for the protection he offered to his kinsmen in the clan.

As both families now joined to discuss the marriage, Pusuh, the most respected elder in the Mongor family headed the family discussions when the Kolloh's came to pay a friendly visit. In such gatherings, the host always came respectfully and sat down peacefully. Fayia, Tamba Kolloh's uncle, accompanied his mother for the consultations in the evenings.

"What's the purpose of your visit?" Pusuh questioned the Kolloh's obediently.

"Hum! I pray that the God of our forebears and the God of our rivers and mountains, bless us all, and to guide us in all our undertakings in our day," said Tamba's uncle.

"*Ameee-nah*!" They all answered together, and Fayia

Kolloh continued.

"That the same blessings shall pour on Tamba Kolloh's head and flow on your daughter, Kumba Mongor's head," said Fayia.

"*Ameee-nah*! They all answered again.

"That they shall unite to bear good fruits like what we are seeing today in Tamba Kolloh, *Ameee-nah*!" Fayia continued.

"Hum! Tewa!" Fayia called Tamba Kolloh's mother.

"Eh!" she answered calmly.

"We have reached this far, and Pusuh has asked us to tell them why we came to pay them a visit today," he said.

"*Balikah* (thank you) Fayia Kolloh," she said and continued. "May the God of our forebears bless us and our children too."

Ameee- nah!" they answered together again.

"I now leave the arrangements in your hands Fayia so that we can move ahead with the other rituals," she concluded with a charming countenance.

"*Balika* Tewa Kolloh, and may the Almighty God bless us all," Fayia said.

"*Ameee-nah*!" They all answered again.

"Well, Pusuh, we came here today because we have found something shinning in this house which we love so much. Our purpose in coming is to "Tie-the-kola" and to also close the door from any other man that may come in our absence to get the very valuable object that we have found in your home. Therefore Pusuh Mongor; it's this reason that brought us here today," Fayia Kolloh Said.

"Uh! Hum!" Pusuh said and nodded.

"*Balika tao-tao* (Thank you so much)."

"We have met before, and I believe that today was just to "tie-the-kola," Pusuh said.

"*Eeeh*! (Yes)," both Fayia Kolloh and Tewah answered in unison.

Kumba Mongor wasn't far from them, and she could hear all what was said, but Tamba Kolloh wasn't present. His uncle and mother represented him. Pusuh Mongor, who was the brother of the late Nyuma Mongor and now the head of Mongor family, represented Kumba in the marriage arrangements. Pusuh then entered into the hut, and hung heads with Kumba, her mother Kpannah, and the other relatives who had come to Yilandu to participate in the historic event.

The Mongor family then questioned Kumba if she was still interested in marrying Tamba Kolloh? She said she was and smiled. Pusuh Mongor, her uncle, and her mother Kpannah brought the good news outdoors to tell the Kolloh family. The Kissi performed all aspects of their culture with a tedious, exact, and a peaceful cultural settlement.

"May the Almighty God bless us all," Pusuh Mongor said.

"*Ameee-nah*!" they all answered.

"Well, we the Mongor family has gone indoors and has hung our heads with Kumba Mongor. She has finally agreed to be united with Tamba Kolloh in Yilandu," Pusuh said.

It was at the very moment that *Yamba* entered the veranda where the both families had sat, and he cried a short and very sweet song. He had indeed been invited to be in that historic gathering, but he had been busy, delayed in the chief's shed, where he had cried during important discussions.

"Ah! Tamba Kolloh and Kumba Mongor, the great giants of Yilandu, and the lions of Toli. May their reunion be a great success in our clan," *Yamba* cried.

He closed his mouth, and chewed a piece of kola nuts he had taken from one of his many pockets. Kumba Mongor loved *Yamba* who always made her laugh. *Yamba* and Tadanpoli the weaver were the greatest comedians in Yilandu. *Yamba* was greater of the two, and vividly remembered to this day.

"*Balika* Pusuh Mongor," said Fayia Kolloh. "*Balika* tao-tao, and may God bless us all."

Yamba again joined in, and the "*Balika* tao-tao" or the "thank you so much," soon became a song. They could hear Kumba Mongor giggling indoors whenever *Yamba* sang a funny song. He was truly a man of great fun, and he never cared as long as the occasion was blessed with food, Tamba Nanjah gin and wine.

Fayia and Tewah Kolloh hung their heads, and Fayia finally brought a calabash of colored kola nuts and he prayed over them, and presented them to Pusuh Mongor. Pusuh also blessed them, and a bottle of gin was brought, and some libation was poured in the ground to their forebears for the occasion to be a great success in Yilandu.

All signified the pleasing of the gods, and the feeding of the spirits of their grandfathers, who remained the guiding spirits of their individual families, the village, and clan.

Some of the kola nuts in the calabash were tied in small bundles, wrapped in large banana leaves, and neatly tied with cords loosed from tree climbers in the bushes around the village. Pusuh then opened one of the bundles, and took a few kola nuts, and broke them into halves. He then offered everyone a piece, and *Yamba* echoed again, at the same time chewing the piece of kola nut. This was to bring new life, and to also show the importance attached to such gatherings.

Pusuh Mongor then folded the huge arms of his country-cloth gown, and sat at a vantage-point on a stool, where his voice could be clearly heard. He thanked the Mongor family for coming and for such a respect paid to them. He told them that they should be very proud since Tamba Kolloh and Kumba Mongor loved each other so much, and were getting married in the Yilandu, instead of them traveling to distant villages to look for a wife or a husband whose culture might be different from theirs.

The families then agreed that the marriage ceremony should be postponed, since Kumba Mongor was expected to give birth to a child soon. Even though she had reached the ninth month in her pregnancy, she looked charming, beautiful, and pleasant. They then completed the process to "tie-the-kola," or engagement in the Kissi culture. The dowry was to be paid later. A dowry can be anything valuable given to the bride's family from the day the "Kola is tied," and to be counted later as previously mentioned.

In case the Mongor family had denied the Kola, it would simply mean that the marriage was annulled. Yet, with the completion of the process, Kumba Mongor was now regarded as Tamba Kolloh's official wife according to their custom. There was great joy in Yilandu when *Yamba* later cried to inform the villagers about the success of the engagement between Tamba Kolloh and Kumba Mongor. That evening, the village drummers drummed again and *Yamba* entertained them until the wee hours of the morning.

Tamba Kolloh, because of his prominence, provided many kegs of the palm wine and bamboo wine. They also had the *Tamba Nanjah* gin in abundance. Food and Kola nuts were shared among the elders in the village, who also prayed and blessed them, and later ate them. The Mongor and Kolloh families took some of the kola nuts to the shrines and oracles where they went to feed the spirits of their great grandfathers.

Kumba Mongor was greatly helped by her mother. Kpannah Mongor had told her daughter about the foods she should avoid, and the ones to eat when pregnant in the Kissi culture. She also advised Kumba to desist from laziness, and to take some short walks that could be very helpful in her situation. Kpannah Mongor was also a midwife, although *Kolooh* was the best midwife in the clan.

Kumba Mongor was again told by her mother to be vigilant, and reiterated her advice for her to avoid eating what the Mongor family considered a taboo – monkey meat. The Mongor Family never ate monkey meat. Any member of the Mongor family, who ignored that advice, had lots of itching on every inch of their body. Yet, it was actually very hard to keep the law. Monkeys were abundant all over in the clan. They even entered in the village, and created lots of mischief and havoc. Sometimes, they even destroyed their crops until the hunters had to frighten, or shoot them down.

In Yilandu, each household sent a bowl of rice to their neighbors. This was repeated. Yet, they all knew the taboo of each household and they informed them earlier, if they had cooked the foods they didn't eat. Kumba Mongor received such offers too. She now grew very heavy, and was tired to do home chores, the neighbors and especially her mother-in-law Tewa Kolloh, did a lot for her.

If the Kolloh's cooked monkey meat, they disclosed this to Kumba Mongor and her mother, and they would then offer her something else. They ate whatever was offered to them. Yet, if one ate one's taboo and didn't know about it in advance, it actually didn't matter in the Kissi custom. However, having knowledge of the taboo, and eating it, was a punishable offence.

"*Ndeh*, why don't we eat monkey meat?" Kumba questioned her mother as they went to weed the small garden beside her late father's hut.

"My daughter, I was told that your great-grandfather decided it. Your late father Nyuma Mongor once informed me that in those days in our clan, there were lots of inter-tribal conflicts, which made our ancestors, spend most of their lives in the jungle near Ngebadu. There they were in company of wild monkeys, huge boa constrictors and other wild beasts. They tamed most of the animals, and when there was a shortage of any food in those days, the monkeys searched for wild fruits for the Mongor family to eat. The family would then live on the food for several days. It was because of that kindness that they agreed never to eat monkey meat again. Most families have broken that taboo in Yilandu, but I don't know why we still believe in it, my daughter. It's not fair in the village when others joke that only the Mongor's don't eat monkey meat in Yilandu."

"*Ndeh*, I saw Uncle Pusuh eating monkey meat the other day, and why?" Kumba said and bowed respectfully with watchful eyes at the same time weeding under the okra plant and picking some garden eggs in the garden.

"Kumba, everyone has their own mind, and should be left to decide for themselves. Your Dad told me never to allow his children to eat monkey meat. You should ask your uncle that question, Kumba," Kpannah Mongor said.

Most families in Yilandu had different types of taboos. Some don't eat kola nuts others eat boa constrictors, eaten by most families in the clan. Some families believe that kola nuts were used to cure wounds in the ancient time, and so, they avoid eating them. Whatever one's taboo might be, there is a good story to tell why you shouldn't eat it.

"Kumba!" Kpannah called her daughter.

"Eh! *Ndeh*," Kumba answered.

"Your in-laws came to "tie-the-kola" yesterday, but your uncle told them that your present condition wouldn't permit the family to undertake any marriage ceremony at this time. A special time shall be set in which our extended families will be invited, as well as drummers and praise singers. This was what we agreed on, and I am only exposing it to you now," Kpannah said with grin of affection.

They then left the garden, and entered into her mother's

hut. Kumba sat on a mat and stretched her legs in front of her. She was really tired due to the pregnancy. Surnah, her little sister, had left her colleagues playing outdoors, and she hurried inside the hut when her elder sister – Kumba, had called her. Kumba had wanted to drink some cold water, and she searched for a small gourd and gave her some water to drink. Surnah benefited from a piece of a roasted cassava that her mother had roasted and eaten from, earlier, but kept a piece for her.

Kumba Mongor now lying sideways and ate a piece of the roasted cassava on which her mother poured some palm oil. Surnah then sat beside her elder sister, thinking that she was in deep pain, and looked at her face sadly.

"A-cho kendia-leh - *Ngore*?" (are you not alright, big sister?), Surnah questioned her elder sister if she wasn't feeling well.

"My friend Sia Fayia and I went to see Tamba Kolloh today. He offered us some food, and oranges. He even sent some kola nuts for *Ndeh*," Surnah said. "She just informed me that Tamba Kolloh's relatives were told about the plans for the marriage, which was postponed until I have his child," Kumba Mongor said to her little sister.

The little girl looked at the thatched roof in the hut, and with her bell-like resonant voice, Surnah said, "*Ngore* Kumba, *Ndeh* and the rest of the family thought so nicely. It was really wise thinking indeed. I also want to believe that even the idea to "tie- the-kola," may have been caused by a special dispensation by both families. You know *Ngore*, our elders don't permit their daughters to get married in the condition you are in," the little girl said wisely.

The custom also never allowed them to keep gifts for unborn babies. It was considered a bad luck, and it made mothers have great difficulties at childbirth. Gifts were given on the day of the birth; unlike western cultures where gifts are given to a pregnant mother before she gives birth.

"*Ngore* Kumba, I really have the conviction that you love Tamba Kolloh, but we love you too," Surnah said with a line of tears running down her right eye.

Their mother listened attentively. Surnah was always admired in the family for being very clever and for the maturity in dealing with her elders. She was indeed a model of her elder sister, beautiful, charming and had great looks. Unlike her elder sister, she spoke softly; breathed at intervals, and was very interested in her elder sister's friendship. She never indulged in wild jokes, and never spoke profane language to anyone.

The custom never allowed children to be rude. If they were, getting a few lashes on the buttocks constantly punished them until they changed their rude behavior. Maybe, Surnah's complacent manner was due to her immaturity and her being a virgin. She was just entering her teenage years.

Kumba Mongor, unlike her little sister, joked with the other lads in Yilandu, and insulted then if they were rude to her. She was feared, and also considered very stubborn and obnoxious. Yet, many of the lads joked with her, and told her that her insults never tore their shirts.

Saki was the last male child in the Mongor family. A young, energetic and handsome boy, he was also Choka's best friend. They roamed the bushes and the banks of rivers where they went to launch fishing expeditions. Saki was always lucky in his deeds and especially in the huge catches he had from his fishing expeditions.

He was among the other village lads who went to swamps in small groups to search for earthworms. They injected them at the mouth of a hook. The hook was then tied to a long pole with a long cord woven from the leaves of a palm tree. Fishing was done by throwing the long cord into the stream or river, and then sat down to watch for the sudden jerks of the cord when a fish had been hooked to it. It meant that the fish had been lured to the hook by the earthworm that was tied at its mouth as bait.

They then drew the cord from the river. The fish that was hooked out fought bravely on the bank of the river to be returned into the river. They were then put inside a fishing basket made of raffia. The fish stayed there, and died slowly.

The night's bright moonlight encouraged the children in Yilandu to continue playing the *Duduleng (hide-and-seek game),* as they watched the sky with countless stars. Usually, the elders sat beside logs of fire and enjoyed the palm wine and bamboo wine narrating very funny and interesting stories to the young.

Many children were always found outside *Yamba's* hut, where he narrated very funny stories to them. Most of these stories ended in sweet songs. Most villagers wouldn't permit their children to play rudely at night. They feared for the evils that roamed the countryside.

At night the villagers discussed the fun shared on their farms, and the hunters discussed their achievements from their hunting expeditions. They believed in the Almighty God, and also recognized the importance of smaller gods that aided them in their daily activities.

The Kissi then practiced a type of a "poly-ethnic religious beliefs," which recognized God, and also recognized smaller gods they prayed to, with the assistance of the spirits for their forebears. These smaller gods were represented in idols, which they adored, and placed them at the oracles and shrines in the clan; but Islam, and especially Christianity discouraged them from such beliefs.

Yet, as the years progressed, some Kissi even accepted Christianity and Islam, but they never forgot their native religion, which served them appropriately.

It was during the rainy season that Kumba Mongor's pains became unbearable. One night, her mother had sent for *Kolooh*, the most gifted midwife. She had picked some medicinal herbs used for delivery purposes. She squashed the leaves in a calabash, and gave Kumba Mongor the content to drink. Her pains cooled down immediately, and within a few hours, she had a safe delivery. It was a bouncing baby boy. Kpannah Mongor had told her that she was going to have a male child since she had chosen an antelope when she and Tamba Kolloh went to see his snares in the forest near Ngebadu.

The constant and lovely cries of a baby woke many villagers up that evening. The good news soon reached Tamba Kolloh. It was *Yamba* who informed him yet, in the Kissi culture, men were not allowed to enter inside a woman's delivery room immediately after delivery. It sometimes took a day or two before even brothers were allowed to enter into a sister's delivery room. It was a very strict law. Tamba Kolloh was an exception. He was a chief priest, and knew exactly what sacrifices to make in case a mother was to have some difficulty in delivering a child.

Early the next day, Tamba Kooloh took some kola nuts and went to visit *Koei (god of fertility*), at the shrine in the swamp beside the Pela stream. There he prayed, and fed the god for giving him a bouncing baby boy. There was dancing the next day, and they drank many kegs of palm and bamboo wine and gin. The child was then named Sahr Kolloh, since he was the first male child.

The Kissi had a special list of names they go by, to name their children, laid down since the ancient times. They were:

(Males)
Sahr, the first male child
Tamba, the second male child
Fayia, the third male child
Fallah, the fourth male child
Nyuma, the fifth male child
Hallie, the sixth male child
Kundu, the seventh male child
Sahr Kollie, the eighth male child (Last Sahr)
The last child is called *Fondoh*

(Females)
Sia, the first female child
Kumba, the second female child
Finda, the third female child
Tewa, the fourth female child

Yawah, the fifth female child
Teneh, the sixth female child
Surnah, the seventh female child
The last is called - *Foowoh*

Interestingly, the Kissi also give names according to someone's profession. If someone is a nurse, they can easily call that person – Kumba Nurse, or, Sahr Teacher, Fayia Driver, and Tamba Police. That is to easily recognize someone's profession, and to make others to easily know the person spoken of.

The christening of Tamba Kolloh's baby was one of the most adored ceremonies ever held in Yilandu. The celebrants were the elders, and on that day, the baby was brought outdoors, and kola nuts were poured in a calabash and prayed upon.

Kendema, versed in such customs, became the head celebrant. The baby lay on Kumba Mongor's mother's arms, and the old man narrated a sacred incantation over him. He then poured a sacred ointment on the baby's forehead, and poured gin on the ground as a libation to appease the gods, and to thank their forefathers for such a safe delivery.

All was done with the thundering of the drums, and *Yamba* cried constantly to tell the whole village that the baby's name was Sahr Kolloh, when the name was finally announced by Kendema, the chief celebrant. It was a joyous occasion indeed; everyone drank palm and bamboo wine, and the *Tamba Nanjahn gin.*

The elders of both the Mongor and the Kolloh families cuddled the baby. The elders then left the village, and they went to thank Koie at the shrine for giving the village such a very handsome and a bouncing baby boy. The occasions continued for several days in the village. The distant relatives brought lots of gifts. Some of them were domestic animals, like goats, sheep, fowls and even Gbekah Kolloh, Tamba Kolloh' s distant uncle, brought a cow for such an important occasions in the clan and to thank his nephew for the good he did for his kinsmen in the clan.

In a few months after Kumba Mongor's safe delivery, Fayia Kolloh, Tamba Kolloh's uncle, met the Mongors, and a date was set for the marriage in the village. Consultations followed, and a final date was set as the rains were lessening and the dry season was about to set in. The dowry was also discussed, and the Kolloh's started to bring the items for the dowry. They brought ten fowls, a goat, a sheep, two cows, tins of palm oil, and bundles of kola nuts. Fayia Kolloh presented the items to Pusuh Mongor, on behalf of the Kolloh family.

Pusuh Mongor now headed the Mongor family after the death of his elder brother, the Late Nyuma Mongor. The distant relatives also started pouring in Yilandu. They came with more gifts. It was an important occasion for their chief priest was getting married. Some brought more fowls, cows, goats, sheep, and even carcasses of some bush animals, for the party that was going to be held in Yilandu. They also brought lots of vegetables and more tins of palm oil.

It was one of the most famous marriage ceremonies ever held in Yilandu in those days. The celebration started a week before the actual marriage ceremony in the village. The distant relatives had been informed, and the *Bolah*, although they were considered the uninvited guests, were the most important people during such an occasion. They too came in large numbers, to attack anyone who mocked them, or stood in their way.

Kumba Mongor now sat and smiled pleasingly. It was also a smile that left her feeling satisfied. As the visitors and their distant relatives continued to come in a steady stream, Tamba Kolloh's hut became a melting pot. People came to seek his psychic advice, and to help cure their sicknesses. He was considered the busiest man in the clan. He went to the oracles and shrines intermittently, and picked exotic herbs most appropriate in curing the different illnesses they brought to his attention. The items for the marriage now filled Kumba Mongor's mother's hut. The domestic animals like the goats, sheep and cows were tied on the outskirts of the village.

As the day drew near, Chief *Gbekah Kondo* called the village elders together. He informed them that they were lucky to have had a son like Tamba Kolloh, and they should do everything in their power to make the occasion a great success in Yilandu. That evening, *Kolooh* was also called, and she started to prepare the village for the occasion.

Drummers from the other villages came, like *Kolobengu*, *Kpangbeining, Maah*, *YeNdeh*, and many others, to join in the occasion. The place was now crowded, and noisy, and, unlike a burial ceremony where most people became onlookers, the marriage ceremony was one in which everyone participated in the dancing and fun.

It was uniquely planned since they didn't have to go to scare birds on the farm. Everyone was present. The dancing had already commenced. *Yamba* was ready too, and he sat at vantage points where he could easily cry to calm everyone down in case the chief or the elders wanted to speak. That was one of his duties.

In the evening before the marriage ceremony, *Kolooh* had gone to the gravesite where the late Nyuma Mongor was buried and had whispered into the ears of the dead. It was simply to tell the dead to bless his daughter's marriage, and to participate in the occasion. She poured some libation on the grave and laid enough rice powder, and many kola nuts, which were considered the food of the spirits of the dead.

Early the next day, which was to be the great day, Tamba Kolloh, Chief *Gbekah Kondo*, and the other elders in Yilandu went to the shrine to thank Koie, and to feed the spirits of their forebears. Although they were on the outskirts of the village, they could hear the intoxicating rhythms of the drums and *Yamba*'s cries in the village.

Kumba Mongor breastfed the baby and felt lively and very happy for the occasion. Most of the young women in the village, and even her distant friends and relatives, came to her aid. They cooked by placing huge pots each on three pointed stones, and dry wood was ignited with fire under them. In case the fire was slow to blaze, they again blew the dry wood with their breaths, or blew it with huge fans also used to winnow grains. Lots of domestic animals were slaughtered. The fowls were killed in large numbers.

They appreciated Tamba Kolloh for being there for them. One that day, *Kolooh* again assumed the most prolific role in the village as savior, and one who headed the scared rites that were to be fulfilled. She was the first to wake up that morning, and ran to the place where the four footpaths intersected and left Yilandu, to the other villages in the clan. She had a calabash on her head, and poured libations an all those footpaths; narrating and singing mysterious incantations, as she blessed each household by sprinkling some exotic liquids in their compound, running from hut to hut.

The chiefs and the elders had already gathered in the chief's shed. They sat silently, and awaited signals from *Kolooh* as she prepared the village for the occasion. They drank wine and gin and some continued to pour libations to the spirits of the dead. The cooking and the dancing went on, nonstop. The visitors were still pouring into the village.

As the sun was spotted in the eastern horizon, *Kolooh* signaled to Chief *Gbekah Kondo* to commence the marriage ceremony. *Yamba* then cried for silence. The heads of both the Mongors and the Kollohs came forward. They were Pusuh Mongor, Kumba Mongor, Kpannah Mongor, and Tewa Kolloh, Fayia Kolloh and Tamba Kolloh himself.

"May the Almighty God guide and bless us all today," Chief *Gbekah Kondo* said. "*Ameee-nah*!" the crowd responded.

"To the elders of the village and the entire clan, we would like to hear from the heads of the Mongors' and the Kollohs' households," said Chief *Gbekah Kondo.*

"Ouh! Ouh! Ouh!" cried *Yamba*, as he tried calming everyone down again. "Chief Gbekah wants to see the head of each of the Mongors' and Kollohs' households! They are present, chief," he cried.

"Pusuh Mongor and Fayia Kolloh, are your children ready for us to proceed with this important part of our custom?" Chief Gbekah questioned them earnestly.

"*Eeeh*! Massah, (Chief)" they responded that they were now ready.

"Elders, this is how far we are now. I am leaving everything in the hands of the most respectable old man, Kendema, to fulfill the rites suitable for such an occasion in our custom. I thank all of you my kinsman, for listening," the chief concluded.

"Oh! Ouh! Ouh!" *Yamba* continued to cry for silence.

Kendema was a man of few words. He thanked the chief, and straight away, asked for the presence of Tamba Kolloh and Kumba Mongor. Their parents accompanied them to the chief's shed where they had prepared some stools for them to sit on. Kendema then stood and touched the heads of both Tamba Kolloh, and Kumba Mongor, with his hands, and narrated some strange incantations.

Each verse ended in the loudest, "*Ameee-nah*!"

A calabash of Kola nuts was brought, and the elders prayed over them. *Kolooh* entered the shed, and put the tail inside the calabash, and sprinkled the contents on everyone in the shed as a sign of pure blessing.

Tamba Kolloh's mother, who sat together with Kumba Mongor's mother behind Tamba and Kumba, held the baby. They too repeated, "*Ameee-nah*!" after each elder who stood to pray for them said each verse.

They also blessed the baby by pouring some ointment on his forehead. The baby's eyes were now opened, and could now see everything that happened to him. He just twisted and cried when the cold ointment and liquids were poured on him.

"Tamba Kolloh, the great grandson of Bandakillie Fugbu of Yilandu, do you today take Kumba Mongor the daughter of the late chief priest, Nyuma Mongor, to be your wife?" Kendema asked loudly.

Yamba then cried the same words in his loudest voice.

"*Eeeh*!" Tamba Kolloh answered positively.

"He said a big YES!" *Yamba* echoed again

"Kumba Mongor, the daughter of one our most trusted and dynamic chief priests in the Toli Clan, do you agree today to be Tamba Kolloh's wife?" Kendema asked her too.

"*Eeeh*!" she agreed with a smiling face.

"She just said a big, YES!" *Yamba* echoed again, and the whole crowd cheered for them.

There was thundering of the drums, and everyone was elated. The elders then poured liquids on their heads, and blessed them. They also blessed the child, and poured some libation on the ground to appease the spirits of their forebears. The rites were then fulfilled, and the elders remained to continue the other aspects of the ceremony. There was now dancing in the village and the dancers went to the bride's compound, which was a bigger place that could accommodate the dancers and spectators. The *Bolah* made much fun, and the occasion lasted for several days in the village.

There was enough food, wine, and gin, to last for several days, and everyone that came really enjoyed the occasion. From that day, the bride was now called, Kumba Kolloh.

She stayed for several days with her parents, since she was still nursing the baby and needed her mother's assistance.

She was finally accompanied to her new home after fulfilling other sacred rites. They were now the most gifted couple who saved the lives of not only the children in Yilandu, but even some elders who were bewitched in the clan.

CHAPTER SEVEN

Most of the youth in Yilandu and in other villages of the Toli Clan had now reached the age when they were initiated in to the traditional bush school. These were called the Poro Society for boys and the young men, and the Sande Society for the girls and young women. The efforts to launch such campaigns were never stonewalled by the chiefs and the elders in the clan.

That year, Yilandu was the perfect site for the societies since their most trusted chief priest was there. The youth could learn a whole lot from him. The dry season was also the perfect time to launch such campaigns, so that those initiated could roam the countryside freely. They could also learn how to set snares, and were taught how to become good mothers and husbands. One of the lessons was to respect one's elders. Unlike the Sande Society, which was camped near or in a village, the Poro Society was camped in the bushes or in the forest at a considerable distance from the village.

They were the joyous days in the Kissi land. The *Tamendoh* (the god of the Poro Society), also called the genie of the bush, drew the boys and the young men like a magnet to the initiation and campaign site. The enrollment was conducted at night, or when the village was asleep. The Tamendoh spoke like it recited an incantation, as the men responsible for the enrollment went to every doorstep: the devil spoke in a very terrifying voice, and the dancing-men interpreted, and blessed by Yamba's voice too.

The household then prayed for their son, and he was led outdoors, and disappeared in the darkness or moonlight. The mothers secretly cried for their children. Only the fathers were allowed to open the door when the devil, and dancing-men, came for their children. The devil then cried by making some faint noises that were interpreted by specially trained dancing-men.

The devil never entered into the house. It stayed outdoors, and women were not allowed to see it. Yet, in some instances, fathers accompanied their children to the initiation camp deep in the forest. Some of the children were afraid to undertake such bold and arduous journeys amid very strange incidents, especially since the devil was considered invisible and spoke in a voice no ordinary person could understand.

The genie's voice made their hearts to pound as if they were robot machines. Some very bold boys marched to the initiation camp by themselves. They could hear the genie's voice echoing very strangely and making sibilant whistling noises. The place was always quiet. The dancing-men knew exactly all the households that had volunteered their children for enrollment and initiation.

Some audacious young men without the aid of their fathers marched outdoors and were engulfed by the claws of the devil, and were marched away. The devil sometimes requested certain things in kind, like kola nuts, fruits, and gin to fulfill the rituals. When the first phase of the initiation was completed at night, the young men were marched in a single file directed by the devil and the dancing-men. They followed the moonlight, walking on a sacred footpath to the initiation camp.

The Mothers were now told that their children had been cooked in a huge pot and they were not to see them again until the exhibition day that was several weeks away. The traditional bush schools lasted for a couple of months. The devil then continued to perform great wonders for the villagers who cooked food every day that was transported by men to the initiation camp. At certain instances, the villagers woke the next day to see many bundles of wood, which they then used for cooking the genie's food.

One of the most enjoyable times at the initiation camp was when the inductees started singing in the camp deep in the woods, some sweet songs in the eerie hours of the morning. Their relatives and loved ones in the village woke up, and sadly listened to the songs with great anxiety and love. They then thought of them for the first time, as if they were with them.

In the case there were other initiation camps in distant villages; such singing competitions were constantly held. They would start at moonlight, and continue until the wee hours of the morning. Each camp sang new songs, and winning such a competition was only noticed when the other camp was silent. It meant that they had no more new songs, and the camp that continued singing was then declared the winner.

Tamba Kolloh also taught the boys about their protection against the witches in the clan. Their hands and feet were picked with sharp instruments and exotic herbs in the forms of powders were put in the sores. The traditional medication stayed there for several days. It was to armor them against snakebites, witches and other inhuman machinations. Graduation was then recognized by mystic and deep tribal marks, or scarifications that appeared on the center of their backs, necks, and hands.

Unlike the boys' camp, the girls' camp was silent in the first few weeks after the initiation. Exhibitions were then held, and the best female shaker players played songs of the Bondo Bush devil. The girls danced to the traditional songs with short skirts made of bamboo leaves, and they each held a tail of an unknown animal in their hand. The dancing displays were accompanied by the tunes of the drummers. Such exhibitions were held for the relatives of the young women to show their marriageable daughters.

It was during such occasions that families selected wives for their sons, even if the sons weren't present, and were in distant lands. During such festivities, the families poured gifts on such young and beautiful women. They cheered for them and hailed them, giving them the assurances that they had been selected to be wife of their son or relative.

Those were the marvelous days in the villages. The singers and shakers players sat on high stands built by the men in the village. There was a particular old man who sat beneath them on a wooden stood and played the samba very well. The young women who had already undergone the initiation of female circumcision were hidden behind the initiation camp. The lead singer yelled for the dancing to commence.

The head of the dancing group answered the yells with a very loud "Ah-e*Eeeh*!"

This told the singers that they were ready, although still hidden behind a thatched door. A woman then emerged shaking her buttocks to match the tunes of the rhythms of the sambas and shakers. The crowd surged to witness them, cheering for them in jubilant moods. They wiped the streams of sweat that drenched all over their faces and bodies with their head ties and farmed them as the dancing continued.

At certain instances, the dancing stopped abruptly, and the dancers were taken shoulder high and praised as the best dancers for that season. The dancers were given lots of gifts by the spectators. The singers and the samba players received gifts from the spectators too. They also drank the wine and gin and poured some libations to the spirits of their forebears, and to Bondo, the god of the women initiation camp.

The rehearsals were held for several days, and the final dancing was held at graduation. As a mark to show their graduation, the girls were marked on their necks, hands and sometimes on their faces.

The graduates, both men and women, now participated in the decision making in the village and in the clan. They had now qualified in their cultural predomination and could now marry, own farmlands, and built huts in the village. They could now gain the respect of their elders. They now knew what the devil was like, and now deciphered the noises it made.

Yet, they kept everything that had encountered at the camps very secret. They never disclosed anything, even to their mothers, brothers or sisters. It was completely against the tradition to disclose such secrets in the village or clan. Even Tamba Kolloh graduated from the Poro Society when he was a little boy in Yilandu many years past.

The Graduation Day was one of the most thrilling days to see. The young men left the camps individually and entered into the village majestically, and as the drums rose to a frenzy. They were now considered to be among the most audacious men in the clan. They, and the spectators, thronged the little alleys between the mud huts; and lovers in their prime waited just to set their eyes on their loved ones; after spending several weeks in the initiation camp, or in the genie's camp, as it were called.

The coffee and cacao plantation that surrounded the village was thronged by young men and young women, just to glance their future husbands, or wives. They ran there to anxiously glance at their loved ones again, as they threatened to converge on them with avidity.

(Graduation time was also the soap manufacturing season in the clan. The outer shells of the coffee and the cacao pods and dried trees of banana plants were dried in the sun and burnt into ashes which were later mixed with black oil produced from palm kernels, and then used to manufacture the *country-black-soap*. It was used to cure dermatological diseases and for bathing).

On Graduation Day, new mats were laid outside the

chief's shed. The graduates left the bushes individually, and came and sat humbly on the mats. They were blessed with lots of gifts from their relatives, loved ones and kinsmen. The dancing continued in the village with great fun and mischief. *Yamba* was also present to introduce the graduates to the spectators when the time came.

These were days in Kissi land when all vendettas and bush cases were settled, and peacefully in the clan. They placated the cases, and the ancient friendship was revered, and solemnized by pouring some libations to the spirits of their forebears. There was peace in the clan again.

Distant relatives and the *Bolah* came to exchange greetings, fun and the antics of old. Children danced and played the outdoors games. The entire village was noisy with the sounds of the samba, shakers, and *Yamba* who cried intermittently when he needed to.

Such festivities lasted for several days. The relatives and friends treated their visitors with special veneration. They danced along with the strolling traditional singers and drummers who went from one household to another.

At the chief's shed, wooden stools and folk-like stools and hammocks were comfortably laid for the elders who came from the distant villages to participate in the graduation day ceremony. They were served, and guzzled cups of fresh palm and bamboo wine. Such meetings were very famous for their friendly gestures. It was also at the chiefs shed that the graduates, referred to as the *Sumuah (young men and women fresh from the poro, or bondo bush)*, were presented to the chief and to the elders by a philosopher in the society bush called, *Sokoyapoh* (*the head of the male initiation camp*), amid the cries of *Yamba*, and thunderous applause.

The graduates were dressed in their newly woven country-cloth shirts, pants, and hats. Some wore short gowns and hats too. *Yamba* sat at a vantage point again to eulogize the entire occasion. The *Sumuah* remained bare-foot. As time went on, they started to wear sandals etc. They beamed proudly. The relatives and individual families paid the fees required for graduation, and their sons were released to them.

The head of the female initiation camp or the *Sokoh*, presented the young women to the chiefs. They too sat on mats, and bowed their heads respectfully as their families and relatives paid their graduation fees to the chief and his council of elders in the shed. As graduates, they had undergone some vigorous lessons on the rudiments of their culture.

The young women were taught child rearing, midwifery, psychic lessons, and cultural engineering with lessons in fishing, home care, dancing styles, and protection against evil spells in the clan. The young men were also taught hunting, which they started by laying snares in the forest; how to become a father, farming, cultural engineering, the making of mats, baskets, weaving, the manufacturing the palm oil, farming and leadership. The young women mostly enjoyed the manufacturing of fishing nets, and the baskets to put fish inside.

The chief made the graduation speeches, and his elders, after the heads of the two bush schools presented the graduates to them. *Yamba* sat, and cried. He was also versed in such graduation proceedings, with an ancient knowledge that had now become encyclopedic.

(Yet as time went on, the Kissi came to realize that such ancient cultural practices were snubbed, as they had more contact with the outside world, with its different religions, and different ideologies. Most of the important traits in their culture have therefore been lost in the passage of time, as the conclusion of this work will tell).

CHAPTER EIGHT

In that ancient time, special sacrifices were held for the expansion of the villages. Today, such villages have become towns. It left a profound imprint on their mental and spiritual achievements. Even today, such relics could also be found in the Kissi clan.

It was how Chief *Gbekah Kondo* founded what is the most prominent town of Koindu today, which is a town just a half a mile from Yilandu, and renowned for its bustling international trade in the north-east of Sierra Leone. *Gbekah Kondo* was the great grandfather of the ruling *FORYOH* family of Koindu as previously mentioned.

The larger the town became, the more it accommodated more foreigners that came and asked the local chiefs for acres of land to build. They built homes, and started to propagate their own religious doctrines and actively participated in the politics of the Kissi. Yet, the indigenous Kissi people only respected them, and treated them with veneration.

Lastly, strange foreign men started coming to the Kissi land from distant places, these practices would be admonished. The newcomers would be Christian missionaries as well as Islamic travelers and traders. By then, the Kissi Empire had grown between three countries which later became known as*, Sierra Leone, Liberia* and *French Guinea.* The strategic location of the Kissi Empire, which later became divided between these three countries through colonial boundaries, is a bustling business center today. It has therefore invited a blend of different cultures as well.

The Christian missionaries and Islamic travelers came to propagate their faith. To do so, they first of all had to persuade the natives that involving themselves in such very complex and very strange beliefs invited darkness their lives. Yet, in the beginning, when the missionaries first came, the Kissi stuck to their beliefs.

The first of such strangers to come to Yilandu in that ancient time was called Abdurahman. He was in his mid-seventies, an irascible old man, slim and tall. He entered into the village with a bundle of his clothes on his head and walked with a cane. His hands trembled when he spoke. The villagers directed him to the Chief's shed.

He never spoke the Kissi dialect, and conversation with him was done by gesticulation. The chiefs and the elders welcomed him with open arms, since they wanted strangers to come to open the village. Abdurahman soon became part of the Kissi, and the elders in the village gave a wife to him.

He kept the young maid as a concubine and through her; he was able to learn the Kissi dialect. She was called *Wangoh*. He built a hut, and the chief and his elders also allocated some acres of farmland to him, and soon raised domestic animals but the people were greatly amazed how he prayed.

In praying, Abdurahman stood upright, and stretched his arms to the sky. He then bowed, and touched his forehead on the bare ground several times. He recited a strange incantation over, and over, with some sacred beads in his hands.

"Bissimilahi! Bissimilahi!" he repeated several times.

The children sat on the bare ground, and put their heads in the crook of their arms and watched him pray his own way. They were greatly astounded by the strange incantations of their visitor.

"Alamani!" he said.

"Alamani!" the children repeated after him.

He mumbled some strange Islamic verses with audibility and Abdurahman soon realized that the villagers didn't like or were never accustomed to such strange religious ostentations. At any time he commenced to pray, a small crowd of onlookers came to see him. He noticed that on all sides of him, were the contractions of humanity in an unending witness and cultural variety. Some of the women stood with their babies hooked at their breasts, as they suckled them, and all of them gazed in amazement at their strange visitor.

"What's Abdurahman doing, Finda?" questioned one of the onlookers scornfully.

"Really Yawah, no one could exactly tell what that old man is up to. Maybe he is insane, off his mind, or maybe that's the way they pray to God in their culture in his home," she said.

They stood and looked at him vindictively until he finished praying. Yet, his lambent humor made them like him. He also joked with them. The Kissi in Yilandu went on to notice that Abdurahman prayed five times a day. The villagers then became bored and never bothered with him anymore. Only the little children came and sat beside him and acted like spies, who later went and informed their parents.

When he could now speak some words in Kissi, he was invited to Tamba Kolloh's hut. There he informed Tamba Kolloh that he came purposely to propagate the Islamic faith, and that Allah was the most merciful and the most powerful.

Since the Islamic faith and the Kissi culture had lots of beliefs in common, like sacrifices, and the conjuring with sacred idols, most of the villagers soon volunteered to be converted to the Islamic religion.

Tamba Kolloh listened attentively to all that the stranger had to say. After which he cleared his voice, and told the old man, the gods of our forebears left the oracles and shrines for them to continue to pour libations on them so that they could answer their prayers. Therefore, for them to ignore their own culture just to please a foreign religion, or to plunge into a culture that they knew nothing about, actually didn't sound pleasing.

He admonished the old man to practice his own doctrine, while the Kissi practiced theirs in the village, and at the same time to remain good neighbors. He definitely reminded the old man that the Kissi wouldn't kill their culture, just to please an unknown stranger.

Abdurahman sat in the greatest fear in Tamba Kolloh's hut. He soon realized that the hut was not only a den for invincible serpents, but also a resort for the highest religious and cultural piety in the clan. They actually never differed with another. They made the same amulets, and they also conjured with mystic incantations. They both manufactured sacred charms in the form of ointment, and liquids from exotic herbs.

The old man could learn more incantations from the Holy Koran. Tamba Kolloh had his shrines and oracles. Yet as time went on, the villagers soon realized that their religion didn't differ from that of Abdurahman, and some soon got interested in it.

Kandagallie was the first indigenous Moslem convert in the village. He was also an agreeable old man, who was easily persuaded by the Abdurahman, and was baptized. Within a short time, the Moslem converts rose to five in number. Abdurahman had wished to see such a division in the village, and that made him more powerful, rich, and his name soon spread to distant villages in the clan.

After several months of teaching them more Islamic verses from the Koran, he felt that it was time to do the actual baptism. He then told them to look for white gowns, white hats, and he was able to look for beads for them with which they recited Islamic incantations.

On the day of the actual baptism, the chief and his elders all assembled to witness a historic incident, in which their kinsmen were going to be converted to a strange religion for the first time in the village. Tamba Kolloh was also present.

Abdurahman was eager to inform them that, "Allah, was the most merciful, the mightiest, and the most benevolent in the Heavens." He also explained to them that, "Man was nothing because he soon faded like a bright star dimming before extinction."

Tamba Kolloh and the elders nodded at every word that came from the Abdurahman's toothless mouth. What he never knew was that the Kissi had their religion, and they even called God, *(Meleka)* and they knew exactly all that the old man said to them.

But Tamba Kolloh was never going to be converted, yet, the Islamic baptizing commenced. Abdurahman recited some Islamic incantations in verses, and he raised his voice, while *Yamba* sat and watched everything with keen eyes in the chief's shed. Abdurahman sat and neatly folded his legs beneath him to support the weight of his body. He read from the Koran some verses, and, and said to Kandagalie with the few Kissi words that he had learnt:

"Today, *Kandagalie,* you have accepted the Islamic faith, and your new name is *Osman.* He then rubbed a sacred ointment on his forehead and narrated some Islamic verses again.

Yamba sat a distant point where he could see the entire occasion in the shed, and he echoed, "*Kandagalie* is now called *Osoumani* in Yilandu," he said.

It made the villagers to giggle, and to enjoy the entire occasion.

"The second person called *Kpakah.* His new name was *Ibrahim.*"

Yamba echoed again, "Old man Kpakah's name has been changed to *Ibrahimah.*"

The villagers giggled again. The fourth person named was *Kendema.* Abdurahman named him *Mohamed.*

Yamba cried again, "Abdurahman said that Kendema is now called *'Mohamedee.'*"

The same giggling continued among the villagers.

The fifth person was *Nyangoh*, whose Muslim name was

Ismailah.

"My people; *Nyangoh's* new name is now *Ismailah.*"

There was giggling among the villagers again. *Yamba* knew how to add the prefixes and the suffixes to every new name that Abdurahman had given to his kinsmen.

At the ceremony a crowd of villagers were greatly concerned about Abdurahman's actions in the village. They thought, about what was in the old man's mind for changing the names of their kinsmen in the village? They were greatly astounded.

It was a decision that was to hunt the Kissi in the future. Tamba Kolloh told the clan that he has informed Abdurahman never to change the names of their forebears, to those of his forebears who they knew nothing about.

"Accepting a religion doesn't mean changing someone's name completely," Tamba Kolloh reiterated.

The Kissi were greatly concerned about someone coming to make them forget about their traditional practices, just to please the gods of his grandfathers. The villagers agreed never to call their kinsmen by their imported names, but by the same old names left by their forebears. They sat and thought over it, with a suspicious view of the old man's plans for the village.

Yamba then confronted Abdurahman one day and said-.

"Hey! You! Abdumhmani, did you come to change our names to those of your own forebears who have died in your country?" He joked with him.

It didn't stay long when Kendema who had been converted, soon announced that he was going to retain his old name, and not the one given by the old man. He was one of the irksome and very irascible, and quarrelsome old men in the village, who sat behind the chief and his elders when they decided cases in the shed. Kendema benefited by drinking lots of wine and even the gin, and growled noisily when drunk.

He had accompanied *Yamba* to Abdurahman's hut, and since he was drunk, sat grumbling with disgruntled gesticulations. He shook his head violently, and in a cold moderate rage. There was already an ungracious dislike between Kendema and Abdurahman especially when Abdurahman told the converts that they should never drink the gin or wine again according the doctrines of the Koran.

The Kissi thought that Kendema and the rest of the converts who had accepted the old man's religion, had sold them as prey to foreigners who were soon to come in large numbers to seize their land. They were also going to make them ignore their traditional beliefs, and their native religion, and therefore make their idols remain shedding tears forever and ever.

By accepting such foreign and very strange religions and changing their names, their grandchildren were now going to have foreign names and foreign ideologies in their heads. They were never going to benefit from the ancient idols left behind by their forebears since there weren't any chief priests to regale them in the glories of the history in their clan.

The elders sat in a pensive mood in the shed. The stringent rays of the burning soon vanished in the hazy sky, and the villagers retired to their homes discouragingly.

Yamba and Kendema thought of threatening the small of

Abdurahman's followers. They went to their various homes, and when they met them praying the same way Abdurahman had taught them, *Yamba* and Kendema sat silently like cats that waited surreptitiously to pounce on their prey and told his followers that by accepting someone's religion doesn't mean changing your name.

They explained to them with a logical calmness that their generation was going to be wiped out because people would never know those who once lived in their locality because of the imported names. They also said that strangers were going to own their land since they accepted anything that was said to them.

Kpakah was one of the converts they met. Although there was logic in what they said, Kpakah couldn't accept nor dispute what they had told him. Yet the manner of his behavior led them to suspect that he was surely going to change his mind. They felt that it was culturally an indictable offense to ignore one's traditional customs, and just try to please foreigners.

But this was exactly what was going to happen in the Toli Clan. The elders were easily persuaded. They accepted God with different ideologies that even the people who imported and preached those doctrines to them. They never knew that every race had their own way of praying to God.

The Kissi later sold their land, and they turned their backs at the idols, that remained shedding tears. It was indeed a cultural mystery. Yet some converts listened to what was said by their kinsmen. They remained loyal to Abdurahman. They surged in small groups and sat on mats in the veranda, with the white hats on their heads. There they prayed five times a day, while Abdurahman stood in front of them and led them in reciting the Islamic verses.

There were also others who agreed to be converted, but never agreed to change their names, or, to ignore their traditional beliefs since both their native religion and Islam had many things in common. The converted villagers continued to make sacrifices at the shrines and the oracles on the outskirts of Yilandu with fowls, domestic animals, and with rice powder that was used to feed the spirits of their ancestors. They also used kola nuts in such traditional sacrifices.

They could also conjure with the idols, and make amulets that were perfectly hidden in their pockets. These amulets did some mysterious deeds for their lives. They were also given some strange charms in the form of liquids that they rubbed and believed to have helped them in their daily activities. They had some mystic powders that they used as charms.

When the population of Muslims increased in the village and in the clan, Abdurahman then called a meeting and told them to build a mosque. It was at the mosque that on a minaret in the mornings, afternoons, and in the evenings to call for prayers. Since the Islamic religion could now be easily translated into their cultural practices and beliefs, it consumed almost the population of the Kissi in the clan.

Some among them never forgot to feed the idols, and they visited Tamba Kolloh, who decorated them with magnificent gifts. Even Tamba Kolloh was later converted, but he remained chief priest although some of Islamic travelers who were well versed in reciting Islamic verses from the Holy Koran threatened his superiority.

Tamba remained firm in his pursuits and was regarded as the only one who wiped the tears of their idols for that time. The Kissi originally took two names: their name at birth and that of the family. Today, they have added either a Moslem name or a Christian name as their middle name when Christian and Islamic schools sprouted in the Land.

Today, Kissi land has flourished with many churches and mosques, without enough chief priests to wipe the tears of their idols after the death of most of their deities like Tamba Kolloh, Nyuma Mongor, and Chief *Gbekah Kondo.*

Christianity has also considerably discouraged them from what they called primitive, barbaric, and polytheistic ways. Churches and Mosques are now competing, and Kissi land has some of the most eloquent and spiritually gifted pastors today. Yet, never will the fame of great men like Tamba Kolloh and *Gbekah Kondo* be erased in their mythology.

The End…

A List of some Kissi Words Interpreted into English

Term	Definition
A-cho-keNdeh!	Are you alright? Or are you/ok?
Ameee-nah!	Amen
Balika	Thank you
Balika-tao-tao	Thank you very much
Bolah	A powerful member of someone's extended family or distant relatives who come

	to an occasion to make it lively with very interesting convivial displays. They are still respected to this day in Kissi land.
Bolanor	My distant relative. (singular)
Bondo	A goddess also considered a devil or genie under whose protection and supervision the Sande Society for girls or the young women is held. The "dancing-women" also help enroll the girls to what is called the *Bondo*-Bush. The idol for *Bondo* is a huge black wooden structure of a female's head with neatly plaited hair. It's also called Sowei by the Kissi and Mende tribes in Sierra Leone.
Duduleng	A type of game played by a group of boys at moonlight in which one is singled out to chase the others who hide from him. Anyone he locates and touches starts the game all over.
Domah	A shirt or a blouse. Also, one of the deadliest and the most powerful of all the Kissi gods that a Chief priest can make someone come in contact with. Its idols are in forms of a ring, a shirt, a coin, a handkerchief etc. This god takes one's life in an instant when the laws are broken. Being in contact with any of these idols, make someone very famous, and very prosperous.
***Eseh*!**	Hi! Or how are you?
***Eeeh*!**	Yes or all right.
Gbekah Kondo	The most famous warrior, gifted ruler and nation builder in the Toli Clan in the Kissi Chiefdom in Sierra Leone. He was reported to

	have fought wars in neighboring Liberia, and in Guinea which extended the Kissi Empire between the countries of the Mano River Union: Sierra Leone, Liberia and Guinea. He was also the great grandfather of the "*FORYOH*" ruling family of the important trading town of Koindu in the east of Sierra Leone. Author's mother also a member of the ruling family.
FORYOH	Ruling family in Koindu, Kissi Teng – Kissi Bendu, Kailahun District, in the Republic of Sierra Leone.
Haa! Haa!	The appropriate yells to scare birds on a farm in Kissi land.
Kolloh	A kola nut.
Keke/ Kekeh	Dad or father.
Koloo-noh	a devil or a genie
Kolooh	Also a philosopher or a country-doctor in Kissi land who is also a midwife, and displays during cultural performances just to make the elders to follow appropriate customs of the Kissi.
Kaelendon	Balafon
KaeNdeh	A traditional musical instrument made from an old iron rod played by a single person by continuously knocking the rod with another rod. The singer sings with a heavy reggae and rap style music. It's played mostly on farms during ploughing and reaping seasons on farms in Kissi land.

Koei	The god of fertility mostly played to at the shrine or at the oracle. This god makes a woman to bear a child if appropriate sacrifices and libations are poured at to feed it at the sacred location. Its idol is in a form of a head of a woman curdling a baby or babies. Any childbearing woman that lays her hands on this idol bears a child. Also, a point of caution that one has to take is to be very careful when buying any artifact imported from Africa. They represent lots of good or bad things especially when one knows nothing about them.
Ndeh	Mother.
Ndeh-nu	My mother.
Ngore	Some one's elder brother or Sister.
Ngufueyoh	A very powerful reapers club still found in Kissi land. They work like robot machines. They can attack, any large farm, and reap it the same day. They are also believed to have some mystic powers they got from a chief priest.
Ouh! Ouh!	The cries of a griot for silence in a traditional Kissi gathering.
Puemdoh	A god of good health. Its idol is mostly found at a shrine or in the home of a chief priest.
***Queseo* (*Queseo-noh*)**	Female singer. Sometimes, it can apply to a male singer too.
Sambeiyoh	It's one of the deadliest gods that can kill instantly. Its idol is invisible. It's said to be in the form of a dragon. It's also considered, bad

	medicine.
Seoh	Shaker / musical instrument
Sokoah	(Plural) –Priests or priestesses.
Sokono	A priest or a priestess.
Samgbah	Samba
Tambaah	A drum
Tamendoh	The god of the Poro Society for boys. Also a devil or a genie.
Tomah	A society (Poro or Sande).
Weiyoh	A type of game played by two players, who face each other. It's made from a cut tree trunk, in which holes are dug. A winner is declared by the amount of seeds that remains in the winners hands.
Yambano	a griot
Yamba	The most famous griot and a comedian that lived in Yilandu village in the ancient time.
Witch-hunt	A traditional war declared on witches and sorcerers who go on an unnecessary killing spree by a Kissi Chief priest.

ABOUT THE AUTHOR

Michael Fayia Kallon was born in the Foryoh compound in Koindu, in the Kissi Teng Chiefdom – Toli; located in the Kissi Bendu area of Kailahun District, of Eastern Sierra Leone, on Africa's west coast. His father the late Borbor Brima Kallon a clinic dispenser was born in Daru, Kailahun District, and his mother, Madam Finda Nyon Foryoh – Kallon, was born in Koindu. He has lived in the United States since he escaped the barbaric war in Liberia in 1980s and in Sierra Leone in the 1990s.

He attended the Catholic Primary School of his hometown in Koindu, and the Holy Trinity Secondary School in Kenema Sierra Leone. He also furthered his education at the Kakata Teachers' College in Kakata, Liberia, where he obtained an Associate Degree in Secondary Education.

He has a Bachelor's Degree (BA), in Writing and Literature from Burlington College in Vermont USA, and a diploma in Freelance Writing with the Harcourt Higher Learning in Scranton, Pennsylvania/USA. He pursued a career in the Basic and Advanced prerequisites in private investigation, from the Detective Training School in California. He has a master's degree in Public Administration from Walden University in the United States, and is now doing a PhD in Public Safety, Criminal Justice, and Emergency Management, at Capella University, also in the United States.

He worked in the Special Security Services at the JFK Airport in New York City/USA. Today, he is behavioral counselor with the Philadelphia School System and assigned at the Davidson School at ELWYN, in Media, Philadelphia, Pennsylvania/USA.

Mr. Kallon has written many works on the Kissi culture, of which *The Ghosts of Ngaingah* - published by Sierra Leonean Writers' Series (SLWS), is his second book, after *Idols with Tears – first* published by Authorhouse / USA, and now by the Sierra Leonean Series (SLWS). His other book, Walking *with a Cane: New York City's Food Stamps War,* is about life's experiences in New York City/USA; also called the 'Big Apple;' and also published by Authorhouse.

'The Kissi Story Teller – Folktales from Sierra Leone,' and *'The Traffic Supervisor,"* were published by Wasteland Press in the United States.

Mr. Kallon is a prominent, and a tireless writer and expect many more stories, and poetry to come. He has founded the *Makona Book Club, Inc.*, (Facebook); a charitable organization to help the Kissi Bendu Communities in Sierra Leone, Liberia, and Guinea, with basic educational materials, and other needs. His website is: *www.makonabooks.com*; emails: *makonabookclub@yahoo.com*; & *Kallonb@aol.com.*

www.ingramcontent.com/pod-product-compliance
Lightning Source LLC
LaVergne TN
LVHW090606110826
845146LV00001B/279

9789988877927